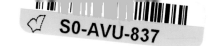

Other Books by Harriet Steel

Becoming Lola

Salvation

City of Dreams

Following the Dream

Dancing and Other Stories

The Inspector de Silva Mysteries

Trouble in Nuala

Dark Clouds over Nuala

Offstage in Nuala

Fatal Finds in Nuala

Christmas in Nuala

Passage from Nuala

Rough Time in Nuala

Taken in Nuala

High Wire in Nuala

Cold Case in Nuala

Break from Nuala

Stardust in Nuala

Long Odds in Nuala

AN INSPECTOR DE SILVA MYSTERY

RETREAT
FROM NUALA

HARRIET STEEL

Author's Note and Acknowledgments

Welcome to the fourteenth book in the Inspector de Silva mystery series. Like the previous ones, this is a self-contained story but wearing my reader's hat, I usually find that my enjoyment of a series is deepened by reading the books in order and getting to know major characters well. With that in mind, I have included thumbnail sketches of those taking part in this story who have featured regularly in the series.

Several years ago, I had the great good fortune to visit the island of Sri Lanka, the former Ceylon. I fell in love with the country straight away, awed by its tremendous natural beauty and the charm and friendliness of its people. I had been planning to write a detective series for some time and when I came home, I decided to set it in Ceylon starting in the 1930s, a time when British Colonial rule created interesting contrasts, and sometimes conflicts, with traditional culture. Thus Inspector Shanti de Silva and his friends were born.

I owe a debt of gratitude to everyone who helped with this book. John Hudspith was as usual an invaluable editor. Julia Gibbs did a marvellous job of proofreading the manuscript, and Jane Dixon Smith designed another excellent cover and layout for me. My thanks also go to all those readers who have told me they enjoyed the previous books in the series and would like to know what Inspector de Silva and his friends did next. Their enthusiasm has encouraged me to keep writing. Above all, my heartfelt gratitude goes to my husband Roger for his unfailing encouragement and support, to say nothing of his patience when Inspector de Silva's world distracts me from this one.

Apart from well-known historical figures, all characters in this book are fictitious. Nuala is also fictitious although loosely based on the hill town of Nuwara Eliya.

Characters who appear regularly in the Inspector de Silva Mysteries

Inspector Shanti de Silva. He began his police career in Ceylon's capital city, Colombo, but in middle age he married and accepted a promotion to inspector in charge of the small force in the hill town of Nuala. He likes a quiet life with his beloved wife, his car, good food, and his garden. He dislikes interference in his work by his British masters and formal occasions.

Jane de Silva. She came to Ceylon as a governess to a wealthy colonial family and met and married Shanti de Silva a few years later. A no-nonsense lady with a dry sense of humour, she likes detective novels and enjoys helping Shanti with his cases.

Sergeant Prasanna. In his thirties and married with a daughter and a son. He's doing well in his job and increasingly taking responsibility. He likes cricket and is exceptionally good at it.

Constable Nadar. A little younger than Prasanna. Diffident at first, he's gained in confidence. Married with two boys. He likes making toys for his sons.

Archie Clutterbuck. Assistant government agent in Nuala and as such responsible for administration and keeping law and order in the area. He enjoys fishing and golf, but dislikes being argued with, and the heat.

Florence Clutterbuck. Archie's wife, a stout, forthright lady. She likes to be queen bee and organise other people.

CHAPTER 1

Sunnybank
March 1947

Shanti de Silva sat on the verandah, sipping his first cup of tea of the day, and surveying his garden. After their usual morning prowl, the cats Billy and Bella snoozed at the top of the steps that led down to the lawn. The rising sun rimmed the coconut palms and banana trees that bordered the garden with gold. To de Silva's left, the vivid orange of a clump of canna lilies stood out against a background of dark foliage. There were flashes of lilac, lime-green, and blue as small birds flitted between bushes on the hunt for insects.

It was a peaceful sight, thought de Silva. It was almost possible to forget that not long ago, the world had been at war. At first the war had seemed so far away, blazing like the sun but, like the sun, not something that he would ever be close to. Of course, there had been many reports of what was going on in Europe. He had been dismayed by them, but not cut to the heart as Jane had been when she heard that places she knew and loved, or that were a source of national pride, had been bombed. Even the rarity of the imported luxuries they'd become used to didn't trouble him unduly. He had changed his evening whisky for arrack without complaint, though happily changed back once normal supplies were restored.

De Silva's thoughts drifted to the day in December 1941 when the Japanese, who had not previously entered the war, launched their surprise attack on the American fleet at anchor in Pearl Harbor. Two hours later, the Americans and the British received Japan's declaration of war. In February 1942 the target was the city of Darwin in Australia where several American, British, and Australian ships were destroyed.

After that, the British feared that it would be Ceylon's turn and watched for a Japanese advance from the southern Indian Ocean. Ceylon had had few military defences but now there was a rush to improve them. Airplanes were brought in, many of them coming in crates from England to be assembled in India. The Colombo golf course and racetrack were sacrificed to provide extra runways, ready to defend Trincomalee and Colombo, important naval bases for the British. If the Japanese destroyed the Eastern fleet that was berthed there, it would effectively close the passage to Australia and affect many supply lines, including some for precious oil.

The first sighting of a Japanese fleet, including aircraft carriers, was made in April 1942. Tragically, the Canadian pilot who radioed it in was shot down and had no chance to tell the British more than that it looked to be located 350 miles south of the island. All other early warning systems failed and when the first wave of Japanese planes came in over Colombo on Easter Sunday morning, the city's defenders on the ground only knew they were close when they saw them with their own eyes.

There were tales of pilots rushing to don their flying gear, jumping into their planes, and trying to take off before it was too late. Some didn't make it, others did, but many were shot down later. There were also tales of men forced to land their burning planes on beaches and in paddy fields, even on Galle Face Green under the haughty stare of the grand Galle Face Hotel.

The Japanese won the day, although fortunately most of the British ships that had been berthed at Colombo had already sailed and those that were left were not of great strategic importance. There were few civilian casualties and equally minor damage at Trincomalee which the Japanese attacked a few days later. The huge harbour there had already, for the most part, been evacuated. The damage to Ceylon's air defences was, however, enormous, as was the shock to her people. They left Colombo in droves, heading for the hills, or from the northern coast, fled to India. Everyone knew about Japan's invasion of Singapore and was terrified that Ceylon would suffer the same fate. Winston Churchill, the British Prime Minister, said later that he thought it had been one of the most dangerous moments of the war.

The British waited for yet another attack, but to their great relief their American allies were persuaded to divert Japan's attention. The two nations were soon locked in deadly combat, and the Japanese never returned to Ceylon.

In August 1945 came the day the world would never forget. Sometimes, when de Silva closed his eyes, he saw the pictures of the enormous mushroom cloud over Hiroshima. In September Japan capitulated, and peace returned to the world.

Jane's voice interrupted his thoughts.

'Ah, here you are.'

The wicker chair he was sitting in creaked as he turned to see her standing in the drawing room door. 'You look gloomy, dear,' she said.

'Just thinking about everything the world's been through in the last few years.'

She came forward and put her hand on his shoulder. 'Terrible times, but thankfully over now.'

'I hope so.'

'I'm sure we all do.' She kissed the top of his head then straightened up. 'Breakfast will be ready soon.' She stroked the cats who had roused themselves at the sound of her voice then started back for the drawing room. 'I'll call you when it's time to come in, Shanti.'

* * *

'Have you a busy day planned?' he asked as he tucked into his egg hoppers a little while later.

'Only some letters to write and a few untidy ends to tie up this morning, but this afternoon I've been invited to the vicarage.'

'Oh? It's not your usual day for church business, is it?'

'No, this is something special. Reverend Peters has a visitor, one of the monks from that Buddhist monastery in the mountains. He's kindly invited some of us ladies to join them. He thought we might like to meet his guest and learn more about life at the monastery. Reverend Peters is really quite broadminded, you know. He's interested in religions other than Christianity and keen to foster understanding and friendship with them.'

De Silva grinned. 'That sounds very forward thinking.' In his experience the British didn't tend to take much interest in the religions or philosophies of other countries unless they had a practical reason for so doing. Jane was, of course, an honourable exception.

'Does it surprise you?'

'A little I suppose, as Peters is a Church of England man.'

'But as he explains, since Buddhism is strictly speaking a philosophy rather than a religion, it and the Church can quite easily co-exist.'

'It sounds like you already know more about it than I do,' said de Silva with a grin. Not for the first time, he was aware that although Buddhism was the system of belief that he had grown up with, he had never studied it in any detail. He admired those who possessed the dedication required to become a monk, but the way of life had never tempted him. 'I look forward to hearing all about the occasion,' he added.

'What about you?'

'Nothing in particular. I want to go over to Hatton. Inspector Singh and I have arranged one of our occasional meetings to keep each other up to date on what's going on in our patches. I'm also due to have a review with Prasanna and Nadar.'

'I hope you have no complaints about them.'

'Not at all, but they still need a bit of mentoring from time to time.'

'Does that mean you won't be home for lunch?'

De Silva nodded. 'I'll get something in town.'

He passed his empty plate to their servant Leela, who had just come into the room bringing the silver toast rack filled with crisp slices of well-browned toast. He smiled at her. 'Thank you, Leela. Are you well this morning?'

'Yes, thank you, sahib.'

'Please tell cook it will only be me here for lunch, Leela,' said Jane. 'And a light one will be sufficient.'

As Leela left the room, Jane reached for a piece of toast and began to butter it. 'I couldn't possibly manage one of Alice Peters' delicious teas otherwise.'

* * *

At the police station, de Silva decided to speak with Constable Nadar first. He looked a little nervous as he came into the office. De Silva gestured to the chair on the opposite side of the desk to his own.

'Sit yourself down, Constable.'

Nadar slid gingerly into the seat. 'Thank you, sir.'

De Silva rested his elbows on the desk and placed the tips of his fingers together. 'No need to look anxious, I can tell you at the outset that I'm pleased with your work.'

Nadar's expression brightened. 'Thank you, sir.'

'If I have a criticism, it's that a little more confidence in your own abilities would be a good thing.'

Nadar gave him a sheepish smile. 'My wife tells me much the same thing, sir.'

'Then it must be right.' De Silva pulled a small pile of papers towards him. 'And there have been several occasions when you've demonstrated it. Now, I'd like to go over some of the recent matters that you've dealt with and give you a few pointers, then we'll be done, and you can ask Prasanna to come in and see me.'

* * *

As he left the station to find lunch, de Silva reflected that with a few more years of experience, Prasanna might easily be the one to take over from him if that was what he wanted. *After all, I can't go on forever*, he thought. He felt a slight qualm as he wondered what retirement would be like. He would have to get used to having a lot more time on his hands. There was his garden, of course, but he might not want to spend every waking hour in it, and anyway, Anif their gardener might worry he was being done out of a job. He and Jane could spend more time together but then she was often busy with her own activities. Perhaps he would have to take up reading detective novels and doing crosswords, as she did, to keep his brain in trim.

It was the hottest time of the day and he had to mop a film of sweat from his forehead even before he had walked twenty yards from the spot where he'd parked the Morris.

In the bazaar, the lanes between the stalls were crammed with people and the noise gave him a headache; he decided not to buy lunch from his favourite stall and go instead to one of the bars on the outskirts of the bazaar that he knew served food as well as drinks. It would be quieter even if it weren't much cooler there.

It was a small place in a row of rather ramshackle buildings that contained shops and workshops as well as bars. De Silva ducked and removed his cap as he went through the low door. He was relieved to find that it was much cooler in the shadowy interior than it had been outside, and there was an appetising smell of curry. He raised a hand in greeting to the proprietor who was standing behind the bar serving another customer with a glass of beer. The man had crinkly grey hair that was on the long side, and bushy eyebrows. He was dressed in a beige suit and a white shirt. When the proprietor had finished pouring his beer, he handed over the money and took a quick swig of his drink before carrying it and the newspaper he picked up from the bar over to a table in the far corner of the room. De Silva guessed he was a Britisher.

The proprietor came over to the table in the window where de Silva had sat down.

'Good afternoon, Inspector,' he said with a broad smile. 'It is many weeks since we have seen you. You are very welcome.'

'Thank you, Manil. I hope you and the family are well.'

Manil waggled his head. 'Everyone is well, Inspector. What will you have today?'

De Silva smiled. They both knew perfectly well that there would only be one choice on the menu, but Manil liked to keep up the illusion that this was a smart restaurant with a menu as long as his arm.

'What do you recommend?' asked de Silva, playing along. Manil tilted his head to one side, considering the question. 'The jackfruit curry is good today,' he said at last.

'That sounds perfect.'

Manil beamed. 'One jackfruit curry with rice coming up.'

'And some of your wife's pickles would be welcome.'

'Of course. Will you have something to drink?'

'An Elephant ginger beer would go down well.'

As Manil went away to fetch the order, de Silva looked around the room. He found it reassuring that in an ever-changing world, it never changed. Behind the bar, tiers of shelves displayed bottles of whisky, arrack, and other spirits, and below stood an elderly refrigerator that Manil used for keeping bottles of beer. A large gold-framed picture of the Buddha, garlanded with paper flowers and its colours turned a little blue with age, took pride of place on the wall opposite the entrance. Elsewhere there were numerous posters advertising Ceylon railway journeys. His eyes were lingering on one that advertised the one that he knew so well, up from Peradeniya to the hill country, when he had the sensation that someone was watching him. He glanced around the room once more and saw that the Britisher was looking in his direction. The man quickly looked away and went back to reading his newspaper.

The ginger beer arrived followed soon afterwards by the curry and rice accompanied by a dish of pickled carrots, green beans, and onions. As de Silva ate, more customers drifted in and soon the little room was hotter and noisier than it had been when he arrived, although not as noisy as the bazaar. He noticed that the Britisher seemed oblivious to it all. He had folded his newspaper up into a small rectangle in the way that Jane did when she was doing the daily crossword and seemed to be engrossed. Perhaps he too was busy working out the clues.

Manil brought another ginger beer and de Silva washed down the last of his meal with it.

'I hope everything was satisfactory,' said Manil as he cleared the dishes a few minutes later.

'Delicious. Please tell your wife her pickles are the best in Nuala.'

Manil chuckled. 'She will be happy to hear it, Inspector.'

De Silva paid his bill and, with a twinge of reluctance, stepped out to the street again. He set his cap back on his head and made his way through the crowds to the Morris. When he reached her, he looked at his watch. It was two o'clock. Plenty of time for his meeting with Singh and the pleasant country drive to Hatton and back.

* * *

'Hello! I'm home.'

De Silva put his jacket on the coat stand in the hall and dropped his cap onto the side table next to the lacquered tray where letters were put if Jane was out when they were delivered. He heard her voice in the drawing room and went to join her, dropping a kiss on her cheek before bending down to fuss the cats who emerged from under their favourite chair to greet him.

'How was your day?' asked Jane.

'Most satisfactory, although it was even hotter down in Hatton than up here. I'll go and have a wash and get changed then I'll tell you all about it.'

He returned to the drawing room a few minutes later wearing a comfortable tunic over a pair of loose cotton trousers and feeling refreshed. Dampened down by a wet comb, his greying hair looked shiny and dark. He went to the sideboard and poured himself his evening whisky and soda.

'Will you join me?'

'Thank you, dear. A sherry would be nice.'

He brought the drinks over to where she was sitting on the sofa, handed Jane hers and then sat down in his armchair. 'I think this spring must be one of the hottest we've had for a long time,' he remarked. 'I'm glad I've no need to go any further from Nuala than Hatton.'

'How was Inspector Singh?'

'On good form. He said things are pretty quiet on his patch at the moment and I'm glad I was able to say the same about Nuala.'

'Did you have lunch with him?'

'No, I ate at Manil's bar before I left town.'

'What was on the extensive menu?' asked Jane with a smile.

'Jackfruit curry, and very good it was.'

'It's lucky I didn't ask cook to serve that for dinner.'

De Silva took a sip of whisky. 'My chat with Nadar was satisfactory too. I told him he'd be justified in having more confidence in his own abilities and he seemed pleased.'

'I hope you had good things to say to Prasanna as well.'

'I did indeed. He's turned into a very capable young fellow.' He paused. 'Although I suppose I really ought to stop thinking of him as young. After all, he's a married man with two children. Before you know it, he'll be snapping at my heels.'

'Oh dear, are you feeling your age?'

De Silva leaned back in his chair and rested his whisky glass on his stomach. It was more of a gentle mound than a table. 'I suppose I am,' he said with a rueful smile. 'Never mind. Tell me what you got up to at the vicarage.'

'Well, it was such an interesting afternoon. The monk who came down from the hill monastery, his name is Soma, told us a lot about the life there. He was happy to answer everyone's questions and after he left us, Reverend Peters said they'd had some very interesting discussions about religion earlier in the day.'

'How did he travel to Nuala? I imagine the monastery must be quite a way off.'

'I believe it's only about twenty miles from Nuala as the crow flies but further by road. It was founded in the time of the Portuguese by Buddhist monks escaping persecution. Soma said he and the other monks usually walk everywhere, but at the moment they have a visitor called Arthur Warrender staying at their guest house who has a car. He wanted to visit Nuala, so he brought Soma down and was taking him back, otherwise he could never have managed the journey in a day.'

'That was a stroke of luck.'

Jane rested her chin on her hand. 'Hearing about this Mr Warrender made me think how interesting it would be to spend a few days at the monastery ourselves. Wouldn't it be fascinating to learn more about the practice of meditation? And then there's yoga. That would be interesting too. What do you think?'

De Silva felt a surge of unease. He might be able to cope with a foray into meditation, although he knew that true mastery of the discipline often took years to achieve, but the idea of yoga alarmed him. If his body had ever been suited to it, it certainly wasn't now. 'I'm not sure I would take to yoga,' he said.

'It's not a problem if you'd rather not try it. Soma explained that it isn't essential for guests to take part. They're not obliged to try meditation either. Soma says if guests would rather spend their time at the monastery simply enjoying some peace and quiet, no one will be offended.'

'I suppose that's reassuring. But I can't take time away from Nuala just like that. I'd have to speak to Archie Clutterbuck first.'

'Naturally, but I'm sure he won't object. It's ages since we've been away, and you've just said that things are quiet at the moment.'

De Silva chuckled. 'Alright, you've got me there. I'm due to see Archie in the morning anyway, so I'll have a word with him about it then.'

'Good.' She raised her sherry glass. 'Let's drink to a fascinating new experience.'

CHAPTER 2

The shutters were closed in the Residence's reception hall when de Silva went to see his boss the following morning. It made the spacious room seem smaller than usual and conveyed an air of lassitude that extended to the white-uniformed servant who eventually opened the door to him. De Silva guessed that Florence, Archie's wife, must be out, or at least busy in another part of the house, or the servant would have answered the bell more promptly.

'Sahib Clutterbuck is in his study,' the servant said.

'Thank you. I'll find my own way.'

As he walked down the familiar corridor, de Silva wondered in what kind of mood Archie would be. He wasn't getting any younger either, and the aches and pains that plagued people of advanced years were often more troublesome in very hot and humid weather. When he knocked on the study door and Archie called out for him to come in, however, he was pleased to hear a cheerful note in his boss's voice. Before he opened the door, he paused briefly. It was two and a half years since Darcy, Archie's beloved Labrador, had passed away after living to a ripe old age. It was the only time that de Silva had seen his boss struggle to control his emotions, and he sympathised with him. He knew what a blow it would be if he and Jane lost Billy or Bella. Fortuitously, about sixth months later, a Labrador belonging to a friend of the family had a litter and the friend insisted that Archie have one of the puppies. He called her Lady and after a shaky start, Florence's little Shih Tzu, Angel, who had always ruled the roost – and with Darcy gone had grown even more used to doing so than before – mellowed and they became good friends.

In the study, Lady trotted over to greet him, tail lashing.

'Damned dog,' said Archie in a testy tone that was, de Silva was certain, only skin deep. 'Always getting underfoot.' He tapped his thigh sharply. 'Lady, come back here at once!'

De Silva gave Lady a last pat as she set off back to her master's side then sat down. Archie scratched her behind the ears. 'Good girl.'

'She's becoming very obedient, sir.'

'Some of the time. I suppose she's not quite two so one mustn't expect miracles. She hasn't had a decent walk yet. I thought we'd take a turn around the gardens whilst you give me your report, give her a run before the day heats up, and that will kill two birds with one stone.' He ran a finger around between the collar of his shirt and his neck. 'I don't mind telling you, I'll be glad when the monsoon arrives, and it's not every year that I say that.'

'A walk will be a pleasure, sir.'

They went out through the door that led directly from Archie's study to the gardens. Where the grass was still in shade, it glistened with the remains of the light dew that had fallen overnight. Beyond the formal gardens, the lake sparkled in the early morning sunshine. Lady careered off in its direction.

'She's a keen swimmer,' remarked Archie. 'Like old Darcy was. No doubt there'll be a flurry of ducks getting out of her way in a moment. Now, anything to report?'

'Nothing in particular. There have been a few problems since we last met but all of them minor and swiftly resolved.'

'Glad to hear it.'

They were passing a small Ceylon oak tree that had

been planted at the place where Darcy was buried, and de Silva saw Archie give it a glance. 'It's coming on well,' he remarked. 'It seemed a fitting tribute to a dog who had a heart of oak.' He blinked and turned away to look in the direction of the lake where de Silva could just discern a sleek black head half submerged in the water.

'I'd better call her back,' said Archie. 'She's had her fun, and I don't want her disturbing the fish.' He put two fingers to his lips and whistled. A few moments later, Lady emerged from the water, ran up the bank and then stopped to shake, shooting spray in all directions. Afterwards, she bounded across the lawn to re-join them, panting and wagging her tail. De Silva hoped she'd finished shaking; he'd planned to spend the rest of the day in his uniform. Luckily, it seemed that she had, and she was soon off again to hurtle around flowerbeds and explore in the bushes, leaving behind her a lingering smell of wet dog.

'How's Jane?' asked Archie. 'Keeping well, I hope.'

'She is, thank you. I hope Mrs Clutterbuck is also well.'

'On excellent form. She was telling me something about a meeting she and Jane went to at the vicarage yesterday, but I must admit, I wasn't really taking in what it was about.'

De Silva could imagine that. Probably the easiest way of living with Florence was to tune out occasionally. But here was his opportunity.

'I understand that a monk from a mountain monastery was visiting Reverend Peters. The intention was to improve understanding and friendship between the two communities.'

'Ah, very laudable.'

'Jane was most impressed with him. She has suggested that she and I spend a few days at the monastery. I understand that guests are welcome. I've told her I'm happy to do so, provided of course that you have no objection to my absenting myself from Nuala for a while.'

A wary expression came over Archie's face. 'Was there a suggestion that anyone else might accompany you?'

De Silva chuckled. 'I don't think so, sir.'

'Just as well. A religious retreat doesn't sound like my kind of thing. Perhaps it will be more up your street.'

'I hope so, but at the very least I'm sure it will be interesting. I have to admit, there is a great deal that I don't know about the teachings of the Buddha.'

'Then you have an opportunity to learn,' said Archie cheerfully. He looked at his wristwatch. 'Well, time I was getting along. I have another meeting shortly. Thank you for coming up, de Silva.' He cupped a hand around his mouth. 'Lady! Here, girl!'

There was a rustling and swaying in a patch of bushes and the Labrador emerged and ran over to them. They turned to walk back to the house with her trotting at Archie's heels.

'So, when do you plan to be off on this trip?' he asked.

'I'm not sure. There are a few arrangements to be made. Perhaps next week if that is acceptable.'

'Certainly. Just let me know, won't you?'

'Of course, sir.'

As he drove back to the station to continue with his day, de Silva reflected that he had no excuse now to back out. Looking on the bright side, a few days in the cooler air of the mountains might be very pleasant, particularly if he wasn't obliged to do anything more than relax and leave Jane to do whatever she pleased.

The dappled shade of the quiet road from the Residence into town gave way to more frequented ones and eventually he had to slow down to negotiate the traffic of bullock carts, cyclists, rickshaws, and pedestrians. He wiped his forehead and pulled the peak of his cap down to shield his eyes from the glare of the sun. Archie was right, the monsoon was going to come as a relief.

16

CHAPTER 3

As de Silva and Jane drove up the narrow road that led to the monastery, the air grew cooler and crisper. From time to time, the dense forest on their left thinned out, affording heart-stopping views of the valley far below. Resolutely, de Silva fixed his eyes on the road and forced himself to stay calm.

He had soon been obliged to drive in a low gear, but nonetheless the Morris's engine began to complain. It was a relief to arrive at the clearing by the roadside where, as promised, three monks in saffron robes waited for them. He brought the Morris to a stop and got out.

The eldest of the three came forward, the palms of his hands pressed together in the traditional gesture of greeting. De Silva guessed he was in his late thirties.

'Welcome! I am Soma. I already know Mrs de Silva, and it is a great pleasure to meet you as well, Inspector. We have been looking forward to your visit.'

De Silva put his hands together and bowed. 'Thank you, we are honoured to be invited. And please call me Shanti, after all, I'm not here in an official capacity.'

Jane, who had just joined them, gestured to the luxuriant green of the forest around them. 'This is all so beautiful. I can't wait to see the monastery.'

Soma gave her a warm smile. 'I hope you won't be disappointed. It lacks the grandeur of monasteries in places such as Kandy. Now, as I mentioned when we first met,' he said to Jane, 'the way up from here is unsuitable for cars, so we must walk, but it shouldn't take more than an hour.' He gestured to the two young monks who were with him. 'Anzan and Chatura will carry your bags.'

The young men seized the de Silvas' suitcases, hoisted them onto their shoulders and set off at a brisk pace on a steep uphill track. De Silva, Jane, and Soma followed somewhat more sedately. The track was rough, and walking was hard. In some places where there was deep shade and the sun rarely penetrated, it became damp and slippery. De Silva's legs began to feel heavy and his chest tight, but he didn't want to appear too unfit, especially as ahead of him Soma and Jane seemed to be enjoying the walk and happily engaged in conversation.

He dropped behind a little to get his breath back and admired the forest around him. He guessed that they must be not far off six thousand feet above sea level by now, considerably higher than Nuala. The trees were shorter than they would be in a lowland forest and many of them were twisted and stunted. Emerald-green mosses blanketed rocks and fallen trunks, and there was an earthy smell of decay. Everywhere he looked there were colonies of ferns and orchids. Unseen parakeets and mynah birds hectored each other in the trees.

After what seemed to him to be longer than an hour, the path levelled out and they reached a grassy plateau. Above it, the upper reaches of the mountain were cloaked with more forest before its summit disappeared in a wreath of cloud. The entrance gate to the monastery stood before them. It was in the traditional style with three stone crossbeams supported by stone pillars. The carvings of the Buddha, stupas, and elephants were not as skilfully done as other examples de Silva had seen, but still it seemed to him remarkable that so much had been achieved in this out-of-the-way place. 'Are the monks the only people who live up here?' he asked.

Soma shook his head. 'There are a few small villages not far away.'

'And how many monks do you have here?'

'Twenty.'

They passed through the gate into a courtyard. Facing them was a single-storey building crowned with a central tower. Its walls were whitewashed, and the entrance door and windows were made of polished teak. From its size, de Silva assumed it was the hall where the monks assembled to pray. Numerous smaller and plainer buildings were ranged around the rest of the courtyard.

'Apart from the gateway, which is from the time of the founding, everything you see is less than ten years old,' said Soma. He gestured to one of the buildings. 'That is the guest house where you will be staying. We have rooms prepared for you. Anzan and Chatura will put your cases there for you and show you where you can wash. No doubt you would be glad of it after your long journey. We have eaten our last meal of the day, but we have some food prepared for you. I'll leave you now, but we'll meet again when you are ready to eat.'

De Silva knew that Buddhist monks ate only twice a day: once in the early morning and then at midday after they had brought back to the monastery the food that they received each morning as alms from the local people. From then on until the following morning, they just drank water.

Anzan and Chatura took them to their quarters. These comprised a bedroom and a sitting room as well as a third much smaller room that adjoined the bedroom. It contained a washstand where soap and two towels were laid out. De Silva feared that the lavatory arrangements were likely to consist of an outside earth closet.

'Shall I bring hot water now?' asked Anzan.

'Yes, please,' said Jane.

'The place looks comfortable,' she remarked as the door closed behind the monks.

De Silva walked around, taking a closer look. "Spartan" seemed the best word to describe the accommodation with its plain white walls, wooden-shuttered windows, and minimal furniture, but at a glance it seemed to be spotlessly clean. He paused in the bedroom and prodded the mattress; at least it wasn't lumpy. 'I think it will do very well. After all, we aren't here for very long.'

He looked up at the ceiling. 'I wonder what we do for light after sunset,' he called out to Jane, who was still in the sitting room.

She came to join him. 'There are some candles on a shelf in there and some wooden candlesticks.' She smiled. 'I think it will be quite romantic.'

De Silva put his arms around her. 'I rather like the sound of that.'

There was a knock at the front door. Jane gave him a quick kiss then went to answer it. It was Anzan carrying a bowl containing the hot water. He took it through to the room with the washstand.

'Bhante Soma wishes Chatura and me to look after you whilst you are here.' He gestured to a bell on the windowsill. 'One of us will come at breakfast and lunchtime and again after prayers in the evening to ask if there is anything we can do for you, but if you want us at any other time, please ring that bell. Only if we are at prayer, we will not be able to answer.'

'Thank you,' said Jane, managing to follow his Sinhalese. 'I'm sure three visits a day will be enough. We'll try not to disturb you at other times.'

'Shall I come back in half an hour to show you where you will eat?'

'Yes, please do.'

* * *

It didn't take them long to wash and change into fresh clothes then put away the few others that they had brought with them. They had just finished when there was another knock at the door and Anzan reappeared.

'Will we eat with you and the other monks?' asked Jane as they crossed the courtyard.

'No, Bhante Soma arranges for guests to eat separately.' Anzan used the customary term of respect when speaking of a superior.

'I see. Are we the only guests staying at the moment?'

'There are four others.'

'Will we meet them this evening?'

'Yes.'

They stopped outside a small building which had a low teak door but no windows, and followed Anzan inside. De Silva had expected the interior to be dark, but it was bright and airy, and he saw that opposite him were two large windows that gave a pleasant view over the forest. The building must be at the edge of the compound.

A table was set for six people, and two of them had already arrived – a man who looked to be in his early sixties, and a lady who was probably a few years younger although as she was heavily made up it was hard to be sure of her age. Her platinum blonde hair was arranged in an elaborate chignon, and she wore a cocktail dress made of dark green silk. The man, who was very thin with sparse sandy hair and a pale angular face dusted with freckles, was dressed in a rumpled suit made of well-worn beige linen. He stood up and came over to shake hands. De Silva found his clasp rather limp.

'My name is Arthur Warrender.' He pointed to the lady. 'And this is Madeleine Moreton.'

'I'm Shanti de Silva, and this is my wife, Jane.'

'It's a great pleasure to meet you both. We've been looking forward to an addition to our little group, haven't we, Madeleine?' He turned to the platinum blonde lady who gave de Silva and Jane a warm smile but stayed seated.

'Forgive me for not getting up,' she said in a languid voice. 'It's been such an exhausting day. The heat, you know.'

'There's no need to apologise,' said Jane politely.

De Silva refrained from remarking that it was a good deal cooler up here than it had been in the valley. He had the impression that Madeleine Moreton was going to be the kind of woman who did as she pleased, regardless of tiresome details like facts.

'I do hope we won't be kept waiting too long,' Madeleine continued. She gave a melodious laugh. 'Although you mustn't expect the Ritz, my dears.'

'Now, now, Madeleine, the food is perfectly acceptable, even though it is rather plain.'

'Plain? Dahl, dahl, and more dahl.'

'There are other things,' said Arthur Warrender mildly.

De Silva had begun to wonder what Madeleine had expected when she chose to stay at a monastery.

'Ah, here we are.' Arthur smiled at Anzan and Chatura who had just come in. Chatura carried an earthenware bowl which de Silva presumed contained the offending dahl, but Anzan had brought a large platter of crisp-looking naan bread accompanied by a piece of white, soft cheese and some sliced mangoes. Arthur rubbed his hands. 'I see we have a treat in honour of our new guests. Marvellous.'

'We are glad you are happy, sahib,' said Chatura. 'Shall I fetch the water for you to drink?'

'Yes, please.'

'The water here is unbeatable,' said Arthur. 'It comes from a spring higher up the mountain where there's also a very pretty lake.'

Madeleine raised an elegantly pencilled eyebrow. 'Only

Arthur could rhapsodise about water. Dom Pérignon would be so much better.' She raised her left hand to pat her hair and de Silva noticed that there was a large diamond ring on the fourth finger.

Jane laughed. 'What brings you to the monastery, Mrs Moreton?'

'Oh, do call me Madeleine. Mrs Moreton sounds so formal. In any case, my poor dear husband has departed this mortal coil.'

'I'm so sorry.'

'No need to be, it was many years ago. I'm a novelist. I come here every year. It gives me the peace and quiet I need to complete my latest *opus*.'

'Oh, I thought I recognised the name. How exciting, one doesn't often meet a real-life author. I've read some of your books and enjoyed them so much. Let me see,' Jane's brow furrowed, '*Death amongst the Dahlias*, the one about a murder at a village flower show, and then *Game, Set, and Death.*'

'Ah yes, the tennis club murder. I was rather pleased with that one. How quickly did you work out who did it?'

'Not until right at the end. It was such a clever twist. Now that I've met you, I simply must ask the library to find me some more titles.'

'How kind,' purred Madeleine.

Chatura arrived with a jug of water, poured out four glasses and departed, leaving the jug on the table.

'Let's sit down,' said Arthur. 'I don't think we need wait any longer for the others. Alec and Belinda are often late.'

The three of them took their places. Arthur picked up one of the bowls that had already been on the table when they arrived. 'A little dahl for you, Madeleine?'

Madeleine sighed. 'I think I'll just have some of the bread and cheese.'

'Let me pass the plate for you, ma'am,' said de Silva.

'Thank you, my dear.'

'The cheese isn't at all bad,' said Arthur. 'They make it here from their own goats.'

Madeleine's retroussé nose wrinkled. 'It's a pity one has to smell them from so far away.'

'Yes, I'm afraid goats aren't the most fragrant of creatures,' said Jane. 'And they wouldn't do for Shanti. They'd soon eat everything in his beloved garden. But the cheese we've had from friends who keep them has always been delicious.'

'Are you a gardener, Mrs de Silva?' asked Arthur.

'Please call me Jane.'

'Thank you, and you must call me Arthur.'

'To answer your question, Arthur, I'm not. Shanti's the gardener in our family. He spends as much time out there as he can.'

'Excellent. Plants are my passion too. That's what brought me to Ceylon in the first place. I'm a clergyman but when I retired, I decided to leave England for more exotic and warmer climes. I've spent the last few years writing a guide to the flora of the island. But I digress, and the dahl is getting cold. Can I tempt you to a little, Jane?'

'Yes, please. I'm quite hungry after the journey up from Nuala.'

'What about you, Inspector?'

De Silva pushed a bowl forward. 'Thank you, I'll certainly have some dahl, and please call me Shanti.'

'I hear you're in charge of the police force in Nuala, Shanti,' said Arthur as he served them. 'I found it a charming place and enjoyed my visit. It worked out very well that I was able to take Soma down on the same day. I understand he had arranged to meet some of your ladies at the vicarage. A remarkable fellow, Soma. His mind is open to everything. Wouldn't you agree, Madeleine?'

Madeleine paused in the act of spreading some of the

goat cheese onto a piece of naan and shrugged. 'You know him far better than I do, Arthur.'

'When I first visited, there were some other guests in residence who had been coming here for a long time. I believe their health prevents them from undertaking the journey now, but they told me that when they first saw the monastery, it was in a ruinous state. Only the gate, that as you may have been told is the original one, was in tolerable condition. I suppose when the place was built in the days of the Portuguese, it would have been very difficult to get hold of building materials up here. It's a miracle the gate was solidly constructed and has lasted for so long. The guests told me that Soma was still a young man when they first met him. They said he often seemed troubled, but eventually he became more settled, and a natural authority showed through. Now he's deputy to the present head monk, who goes by the name of Bhante Gunananda. He's a fine old man but it's thanks to Soma that such buildings as could be repaired were renovated, and those that were beyond repair were rebuilt from scratch. Goodness knows how Soma managed it all, but I hope we can all agree that the results are most satisfactory.'

De Silva cast a glance at Madeleine, but she appeared not to be listening. He nodded. 'I certainly think so.'

'And I second that,' said Jane.

There were a few moments of silence as they ate, broken by Jane. 'You said that your parish was in England, Arthur. In which part of the country was it?'

'The West Country.'

'I might know it. Before I came to Ceylon I worked as a governess for several families down that way.'

Arthur reached for his glass of water before he spoke, knocking it over. Water began to drip over the edge of the table close to Jane. Arthur pulled out a handkerchief and assiduously began to mop it up. 'How clumsy of me,' he said.

He left the wet handkerchief on the table. 'You were saying that you lived in the West Country, Jane. Whereabouts was that?'

'In Devon near Dartington and then in Exeter.'

'Ah, my parish was a long way further west.'

The door opened and a man came in. He looked to be in his thirties and had a scowl on his face. He was followed by a pretty but careworn-looking young woman who smiled awkwardly at Jane and de Silva. Her expression reminded de Silva of a startled deer. This must be the Alec and Belinda that Arthur had mentioned.

'We've started without you, my dears,' said Madeleine. She raised an eyebrow. 'The dahl was getting cold.'

Alec pulled a face. 'Damn the dahl.' He turned to de Silva and Jane with a look that was more of a glare. 'You must be the new guests,' he said gruffly.

Jane gave him a polite smile. 'That's right. I'm Jane de Silva and this is my husband, Shanti.'

'Pleased to meet you. I'm Alec Wragge and this is my wife, Belinda.'

Belinda murmured something unintelligible.

Alec sat down heavily in one of the chairs, not troubling to pull the other one out for his wife. 'I suppose you'd better give me some dahl, Warrender.'

'What about you, Belinda?' Arthur smiled encouragingly at her.

'Just a little, please.'

Arthur served them both, but Alec only took a mouthful of the dahl before he pushed it away.'

'Alec,' whispered Belinda unhappily.

'What?'

'It will seem rude if we don't eat what the monks have to offer.'

Her husband grunted. 'Do you think I don't know that?' He reached abruptly across the table, grabbed a piece of the naan bread and took a bite out of it.

Belinda flushed and didn't answer. De Silva was starting to feel sorry for her.

'What brings you both here?' asked Jane quickly.

'My work,' said Alec. 'I'm an academic, studying ancient Buddhist texts. The monastery has an interesting collection for such an out-of-the-way place.'

'And are you an academic too, Mrs Wragge?'

'Belinda, please. No, but I help Alec with his work when I can. Typing up his notes and that kind of thing. Are you here on a retreat?'

'For a holiday really. Although we're interested in finding out about life in the monastery. Perhaps we can even gain a little experience in the art of meditation, and I would like to try yoga.'

Out of the corner of her eye, Jane noticed that Alec had finished his bread and begun to eat the dahl again, staring morosely into the bowl between mouthfuls.

'How adventurous of you, my dear,' interposed Madeleine. She dabbed her lips with her napkin. 'Now, if you will all forgive me, I must excuse myself.' She put a hand to her throat in a graceful gesture. 'I feel the muse calling. I often do my best work in the evening.'

There was a scraping of chairs as Arthur Warrender and de Silva stood up, followed rather grudgingly by Alec Wragge. As the door closed behind Madeleine, de Silva heard Alec mutter something under his breath.

* * *

Supper over, de Silva and Jane wished Arthur and the Wragges a good night and set off for their apartment. A magnificent sunset marbled the sky with red and gold and the air felt cooler than it had done when they came out to eat.

'I expect it will be quite cold up here at night,' remarked de Silva.

'I expect so, but I'm sure we'll be plenty warm enough. I spotted some extra blankets in one of the cupboards.'

'I'll have to remember to bring the torch tomorrow. I expect it won't be easy to see where one's going after the sun's gone down.'

'I'm sure there will be plenty of starlight.' Jane looked across at the main building. Its windows glowed dimly, and a rhythmic sound like the humming of bees drifted towards them on the evening air. 'I wondered where all the monks had disappeared to. It must be the time for prayers. I'd love to go inside and see what goes on, but it's probably best to leave them in peace tonight. We don't want to cause any offence.'

'Not something Alec Wragge seemed to be bothered about.'

Jane shuddered. 'What an unpleasant man he is. It must be very embarrassing for his wife, poor thing. I noticed that she looked quite red around the eyes, as if she'd been crying before they arrived for supper. I didn't quite catch what he said under his breath after Madeleine Moreton left but it sounded like something uncomplimentary about her books.'

'Perhaps he's not a fan of detective stories.'

'Still, that's no excuse for rudeness. Did you notice how shabby his jacket was?'

'Maybe it's a scholarly affectation.'

'Or perhaps the Wragges are short of money and that makes him bad tempered.'

'At least Arthur Warrender seems friendly,' observed de Silva. 'I'd be interested in talking more to him about this field guide he's working on.'

'I expect there will be an opportunity.'

They reached the door to their apartment and went in.

There was just enough light to find the candles and matches that had been provided. De Silva set three of them into the wooden candlesticks, then struck a match to light them. He placed one candlestick on the small table between the two wicker chairs that the room contained, and the other two on the shelf over the narrow fireplace. They sat down.

'I wonder if we might ask Anzan to light the fire tomorrow evening,' said Jane.

'Are you feeling cold already?'

'Not particularly, but it would make the place look cosier.' She laughed. 'Oh, I know it was my idea to come, so I mustn't complain about missing my creature comforts. And I suppose that a bit of time on a plain diet will do my waistline good.'

The candlelight flickered across the white walls, casting deep shadows into the corners of the room. For a while they dropped into a companionable silence, broken at last by Jane.

'I can't quite fathom Madeleine Morton.'

'Do you mean why she wants to come here? Didn't she say she wanted peace and quiet to finish her novel?'

'Yes, but she could find that in surroundings with modern amenities and more varied food, a luxury hotel, say. I expect she could afford that kind of place. She probably makes a lot of money from her books. I must say, if her washroom is like ours, I admire her for managing to look so soigné.'

'Soigné?'

'Elegant, well turned out.'

'No more than you.'

Jane laughed. 'It's sweet of you to say so, but rather an exaggeration.'

'Nonsense. Well, if she spends most of her time writing, Madeleine Moreton may have to remain an enigma.' He yawned. 'I don't know about you, but I doubt I'll have any trouble getting to sleep tonight. This mountain air is very tiring.'

'We shouldn't go to bed too early though or we'll be awake again in the middle of the night.'

'We may be anyway unless the monks move around very quietly. It's customary for Buddhist monks to get up long before dawn each day. They leave their monasteries and go to nearby villages or towns to ask for alms then come back and share out the food.'

'Yes, Soma mentioned that when we met him at the vicarage.' She rested her chin on her hand. 'What do you think of him so far?'

De Silva pondered before answering. 'I like him. One tends to think of monks as being unworldly and of course there's nothing wrong in that, but he sounds to be more business-like. He's obviously done good work to stop the monastery declining. Even monks need a roof over their heads.'

'I hope you don't regret coming, dear.'

He reached for her hand. 'Not in the slightest, I think we are going to have a very interesting time.'

CHAPTER 4

It rained in the night and when they went to breakfast the following morning, the courtyard was slicked with reddish-brown mud. Jane picked her way across carefully. 'I'm afraid we'll need to clean our shoes,' she said when they arrived in the dining room.

Arthur Warrender, who was already there, nodded. 'You'll find it rains quite often up here, and at most times of the year. The mountains attract the eastern monsoon as well as the western one.'

'Chatura and Anzan will see to that kind of job for you,' said Belinda Wragge, who was sitting next to him. 'Alec and I are always needing our shoes cleaned, aren't we, Alec?'

Alec merely grunted.

'Well, I think that completes the party for breakfast,' said Arthur brightly. 'I can count on the fingers of one hand the times that Madeleine has emerged from her apartment before noon.'

Dahl was on the menu again, this time without any bread or cheese to vary the meal, but de Silva was pleased to find that the dahl was spicier than it had been the previous evening.

'I hope you were comfortable last night,' said Arthur to de Silva and Jane as they all ate.

'We both slept very well, thank you,' said Jane.

'Good, I think you'll find that the mountain air helps one to sleep.'

'I agree with you there,' said de Silva.

'And what are your plans for today?'

'We're not sure yet,' replied Jane. 'I think we may just familiarise ourselves with this place and relax for a while.'

'An excellent idea. For myself, if I'm not going out on an expedition, I spend most of the time in my quarters writing up my notes.'

'I'd be most interested to hear more about your work,' said de Silva.

'And it would give me pleasure to talk to you about it one day, but we mustn't bore the ladies now, must we?'

De Silva stole a sideways glance at Jane. He thought he saw her lips twitch and guessed that she was amused by Arthur's old-fashioned gallantry.

The conversation continued in a desultory fashion with Belinda taking very little part and her husband even less. They had finished eating when Soma arrived to invite the de Silvas to go with him to meet the head monk, Bhante Gunananda.

'Did you have a restful night?' he asked as he led them through the compound towards the building where Gunananda lived.

'We did, thank you,' said Jane. 'We didn't even hear the rain, did we, Shanti? We were quite surprised when we woke up to find it had fallen.'

'It's not unusual. The weather is different here to what you must be used to. If you had come to us a couple of months ago, you would even have seen an occasional frost in the early mornings. The monks are allowed to set off on their journey to collect alms a little later on those days.'

'That seems fair,' said Jane.

'I'm glad they didn't disturb you this morning. When we have guests, they are under strict instructions to leave as quietly as possible.'

'Do they have far to go?' asked Jane.

'An hour or two's walk into the valley. There are no villages this high up.'

That would soon make them fit, thought de Silva.

'Do most of them go?' he asked.

'Usually, provided they are not ill or busy with other duties. Anzan and Chatura for example won't go whilst you're here, as I've given them the job of looking after you.'

'I hope our presence isn't causing too many complications or departures from the usual routine,' said Jane.

'Not at all, it's a great pleasure to have guests with us.'

They passed a garden enclosed by a low wooden fence. It was attractively laid out with neat rows of vegetables and herbs, brightened here and there by clumps of yellow and orange marigolds. At the back of the garden, a bench and two wicker chairs had been placed under a tree.

'That looks a pleasant place to sit,' remarked Jane.

'You're welcome to use it whenever you wish.'

'That's very kind.'

Soma stopped at the door of a modest building, knocked, and went straight in. De Silva heard him talking to someone then he returned to usher them inside.

It was gloomy in the small room. All the shutters but those on the window that faced away from the morning sun were closed. Bhante Gunananda sat cross-legged on the floor; he looked very frail. The large red cushion on which he sat, and the coarsely woven green rug laid out in front of him, provided the only splashes of vivid colour. A shallow brass bowl held a deep layer of ash, and thin trails of smoke rose from the incense sticks embedded in it, releasing a sweet perfume. There was also a small bell. Now that de Silva's eyes had become more accustomed to the dim light, he noticed the string of pale blue beads laced through the old monk's bony fingers. He recalled that it was a Buddhist practice to use these when meditating, to clear the mind and help to induce feelings of peace and serenity.

Gunananda let the beads fall into his lap and placed the palms of his hands together in the customary gesture of welcome. The sleeves of his saffron robe fell back a little, revealing thin arms with withered skin. His face was deeply lined, and his bald head was mottled with age spots, but despite all that, his eyes were those of a younger man: alert and hinting at a shrewd personality. De Silva found it hard to estimate his age.

Gunananda smiled at Jane and said something to her in Sinhalese.

'He's saying he apologises for not being able to speak to you in English,' said Soma. 'You are welcome, and he hopes I've seen to it that you are being well looked after.'

'There's no need to apologise,' Jane replied in Sinhalese. 'I speak a little of your language although not nearly as much as I should after all my years here. As to the welcome we have been given, we couldn't ask for more.'

'I'm very happy to hear it. You must treat the monastery as your home. If there is anything you wish to learn about our ways, Soma will help you, but if you prefer to spend your time resting, you should do so.'

'It would be nice to spend today quietly, but may we join you at prayer time?'

'Of course. We begin at sunset.'

They talked for a little longer with Soma or de Silva translating for Jane's benefit when she couldn't follow all of the conversation, then took their leave. Soma walked them back to the guest apartments where he excused himself and departed to see to some of his regular duties.

'Well, what would you like to do?' asked de Silva. 'Shall we start with a look inside the prayer hall as we're not likely to disturb anyone at this time of day?'

'That would be lovely,' said Jane and they set off. A flight of broad, teak steps led to the prayer hall. The gleaming wood was echoed inside the hall where an area at the back was cordoned off by a rail. Behind it was a shrine containing a golden statue of the seated Buddha that shimmered and glowed in the sunlight streaming in through the entrance doors. It was flanked by brightly coloured devotional pictures and garlands made of paper flowers. The smell of incense was more intense than it had been in Bhante Gunananda's room. Brass lamps of the style that always reminded de Silva of Aladdin's lamp in *The Arabian Nights* gave out a warm light.

'How peaceful it is,' said Jane. 'I'm looking forward to evening prayers.' She took another step and winced. 'Oh dear, I thought I was getting a blister when we walked up here yesterday and now it's really beginning to hurt. It's my own fault for wearing the wrong shoes. I hadn't expected the walk to be so long or so rough. I don't want to make it any worse, so I think I'll sit in that pretty garden and read for a while, but if you want to look around some more, don't let me stop you.'

'I might do that. Are you sure you'll be alright on your own?'

Jane laughed. 'Of course. I couldn't be in a safer place, could I?'

'I suppose not.'

'When you've had enough, come and find me in the garden and tell me what you've discovered.'

'I will.'

They parted company, Jane to fetch her book, and de Silva to explore. Leaving the main part of the monastery compound, he found himself at the edge of an area of rough grass studded with prickly bushes and backed by forest which grew denser as it receded into the distance. He wondered what animals lived there and whether they ever left its shelter to come into the monastery compound. If they did, he hoped they would be harmless. He knew that the monks were not permitted to kill any living thing.

One of the few possessions they were permitted to own was a special strainer so that they could filter water before they drank it to preserve even the smallest of organisms it contained.

A plaintive sound brought him back to his surroundings. For a moment he felt a twinge of alarm but then he saw it was only a small herd of goats. They must be the source of the cheese that had been served at supper the previous evening.

A young monk was with them, and de Silva recognised Anzan. He appeared not to have noticed de Silva and was sitting on a rock, casting a desultory eye over the grazing goats. Most of them were ignoring the rough grass and spending more time tearing branches from very prickly looking bushes or browsing the assortment of vegetable peelings and kitchen scraps scattered on the ground.

De Silva frowned. Up until now, Anzan had seemed to be in good spirits but now it looked as if something was troubling him. De Silva was just wondering if he should move quietly away and leave the young man to his thoughts when he glanced up, noticed the inspector, and quickly roused himself. As de Silva went over to talk to him, a goat grazing nearby tugged a last piece from one of the prickly bushes, lowered its head and made a run at him. De Silva shouted and tried to push it away, feeling the nubbly bones of its undeveloped horns pressing into his palms, but it was a struggle to keep his balance.

Anzan jumped up and came to his rescue. The goat, more responsive to his voice than to de Silva's, shied away and returned to eating bushes. 'I'm sorry, sahib,' said Anzan. 'He's a young one and they're often skittish.'

'No harm done.' De Silva wiped his hands on his trousers.

'Do you need something, sahib? If you do, Chatura will help you.'

'No, no, I'm just taking a walk. Tell me, do you always look after the goats?'

'Only some of the time. It's not such a bad job. They're used to me and don't give me too much trouble.'

'How do you protect them from wild animals?' De Silva noticed there was no fence keeping the goats in. A goat would be a tasty morsel for a hungry leopard.

Anzan shrugged. 'Nothing has ever tried to take them in the daytime and at night we shut them in there.' He indicated a shed at the far side of the clearing. It looked very sturdy.

'A wise precaution.'

There was a pause before de Silva spoke again. 'Have you lived at the monastery for long?'

'Nearly a year.'

'And are you happy with your choice?'

An alarmed expression that changed to wariness came over the young man's face. He looked away, and de Silva regretted his question. He hardly knew the lad and now he had embarrassed him. 'Forgive me.' Quickly, de Silva fished for something different to talk about. 'How do you get water for the goats?' he asked.

'They find most of what they need in the plants they eat but there are many streams on the mountain. Some of them never dry up, even at the hottest times of the year. The largest one feeds a lake not far from the monastery.'

'I should like to see that.'

'Of course. Any of the monks will show you the path that leads up to it.'

* * *

'I met Anzan on my walk,' said de Silva when he returned to the garden and found Jane.

'That was nice. Where was he?'

'With the goats that produce the cheese. He's in charge of them today.'

She pushed her reading glasses down the bridge of her nose and looked at him over the top. 'I've realised who he reminds me of.'

'Who's that?'

'Your sergeant, Prasanna.'

De Silva considered the idea for a moment.

'He's younger of course but good-looking and tall, as Prasanna is,' Jane went on. 'But more to the point, he has that same air that Prasanna does of taking life very seriously under the surface.'

'Hmm. Perhaps you've got something there.' He sighed. 'Maybe subconsciously I was also reminded of Prasanna and that was why I asked a more personal question than I might otherwise have done. I'm afraid I put my foot in it.'

'Oh, dear, what did you ask him?'

'I asked if he was happy with his choice to become a monk.'

'How did he answer?'

'He didn't, but his expression spoke volumes. The question clearly made him very uncomfortable.'

'Well, it can't be helped. If he was offended, let's hope he understands that you meant no harm.'

* * *

'I hope you've had a pleasant morning,' said Arthur Warrender. He was the only one of the other guests to join them for lunch when Chatura served it to them in the room where they had eaten breakfast and supper the previous evening.

'We have, thank you,' said Jane, 'although unfortunately I'm suffering from a blister on my foot, so I wasn't able to join Shanti in his perambulations around the monastery.'

'I'm sorry to hear that.'

'It's nothing really. I'm sure I'll be fine in a day or two and then I can explore.'

'I hope so. The monastery is an interesting place in itself but there are also some very agreeable walks around and about. The mountain lake I mentioned yesterday evening, for example. It isn't far and any of the monks will direct you.'

Chatura arrived bringing bowls of rice and dahl and Arthur, de Silva, and Jane began to eat. As Jane and Arthur talked, de Silva's thoughts drifted back to Anzan until he told himself it was foolish to worry about the young man. He turned his attention back to Arthur and Jane's conversation. 'I've been working on my guide for two years now,' Arthur was saying.

'It sounds an impressive project.'

'It's kind of you to say so. I only hope I'm spared long enough to finish it.'

'I'm sure you will be,' said Jane with a smile.

'I'd like to agree, but there are more than seven thousand species of plants in Ceylon, and hundreds of types of trees, quite a few of them only to be found up in these mountainous regions. I can't hope to catalogue all of them, but one can only do one's best.'

'I expect you're well acquainted with the Botanic Gardens at Peradeniya,' said de Silva.

'Yes, I've spent a great deal of time there. My most recent work has been on the orchid family, potentially a lifetime's study on its own.'

De Silva nodded. 'I have some growing in my garden and they give me great pleasure, but I don't pretend to be an expert on them.'

'To my mind, the pleasure one derives from plants is really the most important thing. Perhaps one day I'll tire of cataloguing them and simply enjoy them.'

'Orchids are beautiful,' said Jane, 'but I often feel there's something unnatural about them. They're almost too perfect.'

'An interesting view, but too perfect or not, they are fascinating plants. As I'm sure you know, they're unable to provide their own nutrients, hence they lodge their seeds in trees and other woody plants and take nutrients from them, but miraculously, they do so without harming the host. But enough of my project. I'd like to hear about your garden in Nuala.'

* * *

'What an agreeable man Arthur is,' said Jane when, lunch over, they were crossing the deserted courtyard on their way back to their quarters.

They had seen the monks returning with their full alms bowls shortly before lunch, their robes like a ribbon of saffron and their bare feet making barely a whisper on the ground. 'I suppose the monastery will be very quiet for a few hours,' Jane went on. 'Soma told us that once the monks have eaten at midday, they often spend time in meditation, then there are prayers at six o'clock which continue until it's time for them to go to bed.'

De Silva pulled a face. 'With no supper. It wouldn't suit me.'

'No, I don't imagine it would.'

'Do you want to rest your foot again this afternoon?'

'I think it would be best. If you'd like to do something else, I still have plenty of my book to read, so I won't be bored.'

'Why don't I keep you company for an hour or so? My stomach feels rather heavy after that rice and dahl. Then if you are content, I'll take a walk and try to find this mountain lake that Arthur was telling us about.'

'That's a good idea.'

* * *

An hour later, after asking the monk who had come to weed the vegetable beds in the garden for the way, de Silva set off for the lake. The path followed a gentle incline to start with, winding between boulders and stunted trees, but then the gradient became steeper and after a while he stopped for a rest. He turned to look back at the view and felt a shiver go through him. Over to his right, the forest that cloaked the mountainside plunged thousands of feet to the valley below.

He reached out to hold on to the nearest tree, one that was not much higher than his head; the bark on the gnarled trunk was rough and crumbly under his hand. He noticed a few small plants sprouting from it, probably the beginnings of some of the orchids that Arthur Warrender had been talking about. It would be interesting to ask him more about his work, although for some reason de Silva couldn't quite put his finger on, he'd had the feeling that Warrender had been quite keen to get off the subject. It was a little odd. People with a passion for something would usually talk for hours unless checked. He shrugged. Perhaps he had been imagining it. As Jane said, Warrender seemed an agreeable man, and good manners dictated that no one should seek to monopolise a conversation.

He took a deep breath, relinquished his grip on the tree and set off again. This time he kept his eyes firmly fixed on the path, a necessary precaution as the stones became smaller and inclined to roll away under his feet, once or twice causing him to stumble. Another ten minutes and he heard voices and laughter up ahead.

As the path rounded a large boulder, the lake came into view. To his surprise, de Silva saw a group of young monks in the water, some of them swimming and others splashing about in the shallows; their robes lay discarded on the shore. It was just as well that Jane hadn't come with him, thought de Silva. It would have been embarrassing for everyone. None of the monks seemed to notice his presence, including an older monk who sat fully dressed not far away from the edge of the lake on a flat rock, apparently deep in thought. De Silva was hesitating, wondering whether to disturb him when the man looked up and he saw that it was Soma.

'Good afternoon! I imagine you didn't expect to find all these people up here,' said the monk. 'We are permitted to bathe occasionally, and this is a convenient spot. As you see,' he gestured to the water, 'our young monks enjoy a respite from their routine. And after all, didn't the Buddha teach us to love and respect nature, and to do our best to live in harmony with her?'

'So I have been told.'

'Please, join me for a while. Unless you intend to go further up the mountain.'

'Thank you.'

De Silva perched on a low rock close to where Soma sat. 'This is far enough for me. I don't have a very good head for heights, and I imagine that the path becomes even steeper as it goes on.'

Soma nodded. 'I've climbed it in the past, but as you say, the going is steep. I see your wife hasn't come with you. She's not unwell, I hope.'

'Only a minor problem, some discomfort with her foot.'

'I'm sorry to hear it. One of the monks may be able to help. He has some medical knowledge and sees to any problems people might have.'

'I'll mention it to her, but I expect she won't want to trouble him. I'm sure she'll be right as rain in a day or two. Usually she's a keen walker.'

They continued to chat for a while, and as they did so, de Silva observed Soma. His shaven head gave him an ascetic air, but he was a handsome man, tall and slim, with finely modelled features and expressive eyes. When he smiled, he exuded considerable charm. De Silva tried to imagine him as he would have been before he entered the monastery. He had probably cut a dashing figure. He wondered what had persuaded him to give up the outside world. Had there been some tragedy in his life that had changed his way of looking at things? Or had the hustle and bustle of the world become distasteful to him? The rat race, some people called it. After his experience with Anzan, thought de Silva, it was best not to ask. He and Soma were only just acquainted. He shivered and realised that the sun had gone off the place where he sat, and the air had grown colder. He knew how quickly day turned to night because Ceylon was close to the equator.

Soma must have noticed the change too, for he got to his feet. 'We ought to go down. Being caught up here in the dark can be dangerous. In any case, the time for evening prayers will soon be upon us.'

'Jane and I would like to attend this evening.'

'Excellent.'

Soma cupped his hands around his mouth and called out to the other monks, who with an obvious show of reluctance, began to trail out of the lake and shake themselves dry before collecting their robes and putting them back on.

'Will you come down with us, Shanti?' asked Soma when he and his party were ready.

'I will, but you go ahead. I like to take my time and all of you have younger legs than mine.'

Soma smiled. 'A few more days of walking in the mountains may redress the balance a little.'

'I'd like to think so, but I won't allow myself to become too optimistic.'

Soma chuckled. 'The Buddha taught that if we leave behind hope and the desire for change, we will achieve peace and true happiness.' He signalled to the other monks and the group set off down the path at a brisk pace. De Silva followed more slowly. He reckoned he still had sufficient time to reach the bottom before the light faded.

* * *

After de Silva had left for his walk, Jane spent another half hour in their quarters. A button had come off her blue paisley blouse and she had noticed a little tear in one of the sleeves, but luckily, she had brought her sewing kit with her. As she sewed, she thought how peaceful it was at the monastery. One was hardly aware of the presence of other people. However, pleasantly restful as it was, she doubted it would suit her forever. Thoughts of giving up the world had never been uppermost in her mind, although she had great respect for the dedication of those who made that decision.

The sound of a door quietly opening and closing roused her from her musings. She'd noticed that Madeleine Moreton occupied the rooms beyond theirs; she must be going out. Idly, Jane wondered where she was going to. She had missed lunch as well as breakfast. Either she was one of those women who, out of concern for keeping their figure, rarely ate, or something was served to her in her apartment.

Jane put in the last row of neat, tiny stitches, knotted the cotton thread, and snipped it off. She folded the blouse on the bed and put it away in one of the drawers. Even though the window overlooking the courtyard was open, it was becoming stuffy in the room. She would take her book out to the garden and read there for a while.

Madeleine hadn't gone far. As Jane approached the garden, she saw her sitting in one of the chairs in the shady corner. She wore a large green sunhat and a white kaftan embroidered with green and gold silk thread. Chunky gold bangles, a rope of pearls, and a gold brooch in the shape of a snake with ruby eyes completed the outfit. *Much better suited to the French Riviera than a Buddhist monastery*, thought Jane with amusement. Pen in hand, Madeleine seemed engrossed in the pile of papers she was reading and didn't look up until Jane lifted the latch of the garden gate.

'Ah, Jane. Are you coming to join me?'

'If you don't mind, but please don't let me disturb you. You look busy.'

'Only doing a little editing. It was too hot in my room.' Madeleine sighed. 'I'm afraid the monastery doesn't run to ceiling fans.'

'Our room has the same problem, but it was cool last night.'

She sat down in the chair next to Madeleine's, noticing that the sheet of paper on top of the pile was covered in spikey black writing. There were several crossings out and notes had been written in the margin with a blue pen in a much more rounded hand.

Madeleine reached for the canvas bag at her feet and slipped the bundle of papers into it. 'I'm glad of a rest. I've been hard at work all morning.' She smiled. 'Writing is hard work, you know. I'm sure many people think it's as easy as pie.'

'I promise I'm not one of them,' replied Jane with a smile. 'I've often wondered how authors do it. Creating all those plots and characters and making them come alive. I'm sure I should run out of ideas in no time.'

Madeleine laughed. 'Oh, I run out of ideas all the time, or at least I have the ideas then find they don't work. The answer is usually a good walk or a cup of tea. The secret to writing, as it is to so many things, is ten per cent inspiration and ninety per cent perspiration.'

Jane could imagine Madeleine sipping tea from a delicate bone china cup, or perhaps an exotic rose-pink

Moroccan tea glass decorated with gold arabesques, but it was hard to visualise her rambling over hills and dales.

'What have you done with your husband this afternoon?'

'Shanti's gone for a walk. He wanted to visit the lake that Arthur told us about.'

'Ah yes, it's a charming spot.'

'I'd like to visit it myself but I'm suffering from a blister on my foot, and I'd rather wait until it's healed up.'

'Very wise. One doesn't want to get an infection in this heat.' A wistful expression flitted over Madeleine's face. 'My late husband and I never came here together.'

'Have you been widowed for long?' asked Jane gently.

'George died five years ago — a heart attack. He was sixty, ten years older than me.'

'I'm so sorry.'

'Thank you, my dear. I'm very lucky that I have my books to write. It means I'm never idle. And of course,' she gave Jane a mischievous smile, 'one never knows what's around the corner.'

* * *

'Did you enjoy your walk?' asked Jane when de Silva found her back in their sitting room.

'Yes, and I had an unexpected encounter.'

'Oh?'

He told her about meeting Soma and the other monks up at the lake.

'I'm glad they're allowed to have fun sometimes. I don't suppose Anzan and Chatura were with them.'

'Not that I noticed.'

'I hope they weren't prevented from joining in on our account, particularly Anzan if he needs cheering up. I know they've been told they must be available in case we want something, but it's not as if we need attention all the time.'

De Silva gave her a stern look. 'I hope you're not going to start worrying about Anzan.'

'Of course I'm not, but entering a monastery is a big decision for any man to make, especially one as young as he is. If he's regretting it, I hope he'll act on that.'

'It was good to have the chance to talk more with Soma. I didn't want to pry but I'd be interested to know what led him to take up the monastic life.'

'Perhaps if we get to know him a little better there will be an opportunity to ask.'

'Maybe.'

'Well, I had an interesting encounter too. I went to the garden to read and met Madeleine. She was doing some work on her next book, but she stopped, and we chatted for a while. I came away thinking that she's very likeable, and much more down to earth than her manner suggested yesterday evening. She told me she's been a widow for five years and her writing has been a great consolation to her.'

'I expect it has.'

'Then we had a lovely chat about books, detective novels in particular.'

'I'm glad you had an interesting afternoon.' De Silva looked at his watch. 'Now, it's nearly six o'clock. If we're going to attend prayers, we should be on our way.'

'Just give me a moment to find something to cover my hair then I'll be ready.'

* * *

The last vestiges of the sunset were fading from the sky as they walked to the prayer hall. The carved, polished teak doors stood open, and a warm light emanated from within. De Silva and Jane mounted the stairs and slipped in at the back. By lamplight, the hall's appearance was very

47

different from what it had been during the day. Illuminated by hundreds of small butter lamps, the shrine glowed, and the richly coloured wall hangings took on a deeper hue. The ceiling was filled with mysterious shadows. De Silva breathed in the scent of sandalwood.

A group of monks knelt before the shrine, separated from onlookers by wooden railings. It was hard to believe that the young ones, now so quiet and reverent, were the same young men who had been larking about at the lake that afternoon. De Silva's mind went back to his conversation with Soma. It hadn't occurred to him at the time, but now it did, that Soma's remark about Buddha's teaching on giving up hope and the desire for change to achieve true happiness had been rather an odd thing for him to say. Hadn't Arthur told them that it was Soma who had taken the monastery in hand to arrest its decline? De Silva wondered how he squared that with giving up the desire for change. *But then*, he thought, *perhaps I haven't understood the teaching correctly*.

Jane nudged him. 'Madeleine is here and Arthur, but no sign of the Wragges,' she whispered.

'It's not compulsory to attend,' de Silva whispered back.

A bell tinkled and Bhante Gunananda began to speak, reciting the opening prayers. Some of the words were familiar to de Silva. As the other monks joined in, the sound swelled. He felt a sense of peace come over him as he listened to the rhythmic chanting. The effect was almost hypnotic; he bowed his head and let his mind float free, thoughts of Soma forgotten.

CHAPTER 5

The next few days passed with little to mark them out from each other. The peaceful monastic routine was one that de Silva found surprisingly easy to slip into. He talked with some of the monks and learned more about their lives and the teachings of the Buddha. He also continued to explore his surroundings and when her foot recovered, Jane joined him from time to time. At her instigation, when one of the monks offered to give them some instruction in yoga he even attempted it, but after a short time decided that, as he had anticipated, it was too much of a challenge for him. Meditation had been a different matter. He hadn't found it easy, but he felt he had eventually achieved some success.

'I think it would take a long time to really master the skill,' he said when he and Jane talked about it on one of their walks to the lake. 'But at our latest attempt, I did have the sensation that my mind quietened.'

'I know what you mean. All the usual little cares and concerns seemed to slip away, even if it was only for a short while. Perhaps we should make a point of keeping up the practice at home.'

'Yes, we should.'

They reached the lake and sat down on a rock near the edge. This time there were no monks swimming, and the water was inky black and still.

'I hope you're not tired of being here,' said Jane.

'Not in the least. It's a beautiful place and the mountain air is invigorating. I enjoy the company of Arthur Warrender too, although, apart from that first lunchtime when he told us a little about it, he still doesn't seem very forthcoming about his work.'

'Understandable perhaps, as we usually meet him at mealtimes. Presumably, he's still concerned that ladies can only cope with a little bit of talk about serious subjects before they become terribly confused and bored.'

De Silva chuckled. 'Do you mean to say that isn't the case?'

Jane gave him a scowl and pinched his arm.

'Ouch!' He rubbed the place. 'Well, I suppose I deserved that. And then I'm always intrigued to see what Madeleine Moreton will emerge from her apartment wearing next.'

Jane giggled. 'Yes, she does seem to own a lot of fashionable clothes.'

'I must admit though that I miss cook's good meals. A pea and cashew curry would go down very well. Endless rice and dahl do become wearisome. On that I have to agree with Alec Wragge.'

Jane looked thoughtful. 'We've hardly spoken to the Wragges since that first evening.' She sighed. 'And when I see them, they don't look happy together. It's such a shame. They're both so young. I doubt they've been married for long.'

De Silva put his arm around her shoulders. 'I'm constantly reminded that I'm a very lucky man.'

Jane kissed his cheek. 'Thank you, dear. I'm lucky too.'

They sat for a short while longer, enjoying the scenery, until the sun was low in the sky.

'We should go down,' said Jane. 'I don't want to negotiate that path in the dark.'

'Definitely not. I haven't even got the torch I brought from the car. I left it in our quarters.'

They were halfway back to the monastery when they heard voices. Jane paused. 'I wonder where they're coming from,' she said. 'I don't remember seeing another path on the way up.'

'Over the last few days, I have noticed a few places where there might be diversions from the main path, but I wouldn't like to take a chance that any of them would lead to places where we would want to go.'

'I hope no one's in trouble. Should we try to find out more?'

De Silva listened again. 'It doesn't sound as if there's anyone in distress. Who knows? It might have been some of those goats. They can sound very human, you know, and Anzan mentioned something about them straying onto the mountainside occasionally, although he said they always return before nightfall.'

'All the same, if we do see any goats, we ought to find him and tell him where they are.'

They continued down the rocky path and were not far from the bottom when they saw a man dressed in saffron robes ahead of them. He was tall and walked with a purposeful stride.

'I think that's Soma,' said Jane with a frown. 'It was probably him on the mountain, although I could swear that I heard two voices.'

Soma must have heard her, for he turned. He waited for them to catch up and put his hands together in greeting. 'Have you come from the lake?'

'Yes, but we didn't stay long. We didn't want to get caught on the mountain in the dark.'

'I agree that would be unwise. It's easy to have an accident.'

'We didn't see you there. Were you doing a different walk?'

'Yes, there are several, but unless you know the mountain well, I don't recommend attempting them.'

'We thought we heard voices and wondered if there were other walkers out, or perhaps some of the goats had gone astray. They can sound so human, can't they?'

Soma shrugged. 'I didn't see any goats, but of course they are agile enough to end up in places that humans have no chance of reaching. It never ceases to amaze me. Fortunately, they usually find their way home before dark and it's a long time since we've lost one. As to human voices, I've been walking alone. Perhaps if not goats, it was some other animals or birds, or even the wind that you heard. Up here it plays tricks on the ears.' He cleared his throat. 'Now, please forgive me but I must hurry along. I have much to do before prayers begin.'

De Silva and Jane bid him farewell and continued to descend the path. Ahead of them, Soma's tall athletic figure soon disappeared.

'Do you think there was something rather odd about his suggestions?' asked Jane.

'How do you mean?'

'Well, there isn't much wind. In fact it's really very still, and we've observed before that one doesn't hear birds up here. Apart from a few stunted trees and prickly bushes, there isn't much in the way of vegetation. Why would birds come up here when they have a forest down below offering shelter and plenty of food?'

De Silva nodded. 'That's a fair point.'

'As for animals, what would live up here? The most likely creatures would be rodents or snakes.'

De Silva shuddered. He didn't mind rodents as long as they didn't come in the house, but snakes were a different matter. 'I suppose his suggestions do seem rather unlikely, but maybe not impossible. After all, what could he possibly be hiding?'

* * *

'We must hurry, or we'll be late for dinner,' said Jane when they reached the monastery. 'I feel quite weary this evening. Shall we just have a rest after we've eaten and not attend prayers?'

'I'm happy with that.'

Whilst he washed in their quarters, de Silva's mind turned wistfully to the pre-prandial whisky and soda that he might have been enjoying if he were back at Sunnybank.

'I wonder how Billy and Bella are getting on,' he called out to Jane who was in the bedroom brushing her hair.

'I'm sure Delisha and the others are looking after them very well. They're probably not missing us at all.'

He grinned. 'I hope they're missing us just a little bit.'

'Well, we haven't all that long now before we leave. The time has really flown.'

'You've been busier than I have with your yoga.'

'I'm sorry you didn't take to it, but I'm sure that the fresh air and exercise has done you good.'

'Yes, it has, but it will be good to be home. It's been a most interesting visit, but as the saying goes, *east or west, home is best*.' De Silva stretched his arms above his head and yawned. 'My goodness, this mountain air is very tiring. I'll need another holiday soon. I hope Prasanna and Nadar have been keeping up to date at the station. I don't want to find a pile of work on my desk.'

Jane laughed. 'I expect they have. Anyway, you said everything was quiet in Nuala when we left.'

'Yes, it was.'

They were on their way to have dinner when they saw Alec and Belinda Wragge coming out of the prayer hall.

'I hope they saw the flowers,' said Jane. 'I popped in this morning and the fresh ones around the shrine were very beautiful.'

'They don't look as if they've been doing anything as enjoyable as admiring flowers.'

It was clear that the Wragges hadn't seen them. They were deep in conversation, at least Alec Wragge was talking, jabbing the air with a finger as if to emphasise his points. Belinda wasn't looking at him, and her shoulders were hunched. She reminded de Silva of an animal cowering away from its master because it feared a blow. It was clear that she was extremely distressed.

De Silva was just wondering whether he should intervene when she broke away, brushing off the hand her husband put out to try to detain her. He made as if to follow then hesitated. A moment later, he noticed the de Silvas.

'Oh dear,' said Jane. 'How embarrassing. We'll just have to pretend that we haven't noticed anything out of the ordinary going on.'

Alec slouched over to them, his face red, and his expression discomfited. 'Belinda's not feeling well this evening,' he grunted. 'She's decided to give supper a miss.'

'Nothing serious, I hope,' said Jane kindly.

'I shouldn't think so. She'll probably be fine in the morning.' He looked away.

'Well,' said Jane brightly. 'Shall we go to the dining room?'

Alec was even more silent than usual throughout the meal, tearing apart the naan bread served with the rice and dahl as if it were his mortal enemy. When he had finished his food, he gulped down a glass of water and excused himself, mumbling something about going to see if Belinda was feeling better.

'My goodness, what was all that about?' asked Madeleine. 'Alec's never exactly brimming with charm, but this evening he was even worse than usual. And are we really supposed to believe that Belinda is unwell? I spoke to her this afternoon. She looked fine to me and didn't mention anything.'

'It might be a sudden indisposition, I suppose,' said Arthur.

'Nonsense. The only thing Belinda's suffering from is a dreadful husband. I can't remember when I've met a more obnoxious man than Alec. He once had the nerve to describe my books as puerile. Oh, not to my face, but in my hearing and I'm convinced he knew it. If I were Belinda, I'd get rid of him as soon as the opportunity arose.'

'Life's not always as easy as that, Madeleine,' said Arthur mildly.

Madeleine scowled at him. 'Well, if she should ever ask my opinion, I'll give it to her.'

Jane rather hoped Belinda wouldn't. Few women were as independent as Madeleine, and she might only make matters worse. She did seem to be in a particularly combative mood tonight. Jane wondered why.

CHAPTER 6

The following morning, disturbed by the muted sounds of the monks rising to begin their day, de Silva woke from a light sleep. It was still dark, but even though he turned over and tried to settle down again, he soon realised that he was now too awake to manage it. One of the things he had been wanting to do was see the sunrise from the vantage point of the lake, but so far he hadn't woken in time or when he had, sleep had seemed the more attractive option. There would be a few more opportunities after this one, but there was no time like the present. He decided to go now.

Beside him, Jane stirred. 'What's the matter?'

'Nothing. I'm going to walk up to the lake to catch the sunrise. Would you like to come?'

'No, thank you, I'm more than happy for you to tell me about it.' She rolled over and closed her eyes.

De Silva reached for his wristwatch that he had left on the bedside table the night before. He squinted at the hands; it was just after five. He had better hurry; the sun rose as quickly as it set in Ceylon. He pulled on warm clothes and a pair of shoes then ran his fingers through his hair to tidy it. It would do. There would be no one up there to see him anyway.

'Don't forget to take the torch,' mumbled Jane, still half asleep. 'You can use it to see if there are any snakes to avoid.'

'We haven't seen any up there yet. If we had, I wouldn't

be going, but I'll take it.' He fumbled around on the top of the chest of drawers until his hand met the torch. 'I won't be long.'

There was no sound from the rest of the guest quarters as he let himself out of his and Jane's door onto the verandah that separated the building from the courtyard. He wondered if Alec and Belinda Wragge had made up after their quarrel. When he and Jane had returned to their quarters after supper the previous night, there had been no noise from their room. There was a chill in the air, and he was glad of his jacket. As he passed the last of the monks setting off on their daily excursion for alms, he exchanged nods and smiles with them.

Reaching the bottom of the path to the lake, he shone the beam of the torch on the ground in front of him to give himself the best chance of negotiating the uneven surface without any mishaps. The sky was already turning from black to slate grey. He hoped he hadn't left it too late. He was glad to find that he didn't need to stop for a rest. The gradient seemed far less formidable than it had done when he'd first attempted it.

The lake looked dark and mysterious with a breath of mist floating just above the surface; it was understandable that the ancients had believed such places to be inhabited by monsters or sprites. He shivered, then reminded himself that this was the twentieth century, and such beings were myths that only existed between the pages of books. Snakes, however, were a different matter. He swept the torch beam around, careful to shine light into every crevice and hollow before he perched himself on the flat rock where Soma had sat. There, he made himself comfortable and waited, looking to the east. The sky arching over him seemed vast. The moon had set but a few stars were still visible although their light was fading fast as the slate grey of the sky changed to a paler shade and then to pearl.

A slender curve of flaming orange pulsed on the horizon, growing broader as the sun rose. The undersides of the few clouds that drifted across the sky glowed like burning coals. A few moments more and the sky was a vibrant orange. De Silva felt a thrill of wonder. It was a great pity that Jane hadn't come with him. It was impossible to do justice in words to such beauty.

He continued to watch but the best of the sunrise soon faded. The sheen of mist on the surface of the lake remained but the water had lost its mysterious quality. He hauled himself to his feet and rubbed his sides. Hopefully, the walk down would take away the stiffness that his rocky seat had brought on. He looked around him and felt a little sad; he doubted he would see this place again. He was glad that Jane had persuaded him to come. It was good to leave one's familiar environment behind sometimes.

As he picked his way down the steep section of the path, the light was still dim, but a movement in the periphery of his vision attracted his attention. Someone looked to be following a different path that came in from his left, curving around the mountain about a hundred feet lower down. He stopped to watch then realised that there were two people there, both dressed in dark clothing. Their paths diverged, and the taller of the two disappeared over the brow of a low outcrop of rock. The other one was visible for longer but then de Silva lost sight of them too as they went into a clump of trees. Puzzled, he continued to descend. As he had been uphill of both people when he saw them and they had not looked back, he was fairly sure they hadn't noticed him, but he was pretty certain that he recognised them. If he was right, what were Madeleine Moreton and Soma doing out on the mountainside together, especially at such an early hour?

* * *

59

Jane was sitting up in bed when he returned to their apartment. 'You were a long time,' she said. 'I was beginning to worry.'

'I deliberately went slowly on the way down.'

'You look perplexed. Has something happened?'

'If it was Madeleine and Soma, I didn't want to run into them,' he finished after he had explained what he'd seen.

'I'm sure you didn't. It sounds like it would have been embarrassing for all of you. Whatever do you think they would have been doing up there?'

'That's the question I've been asking myself.'

'I know Madeleine is an unconventional person,' said Jane with a frown, 'but Soma is in a position of authority here and has taken vows. Why take the risk of being seen together in such a way and causing comment?'

'I agree.'

'There has to be a compelling reason.' Jane paused. 'And at the moment, I can only think of one.'

'Do you mean a romantic involvement?'

'Yes. Perhaps they'd argued and that was why Madeleine was in such a bad mood at dinner yesterday evening. Maybe they met this morning because they wanted to make up.' She sighed. 'If I'm right, I feel sorry for them. They're likely to have even harder hill to climb than we did.'

'I'm afraid so.' He hadn't turned his mind to it before, but now he wondered what the other guests at the monastery thought about the marriage between him and Jane. By now in Nuala, most people took it in their stride, but elsewhere it might not be the case. If any of them did disapprove, however, they were either too polite, or too preoccupied with their own affairs, to show it.

* * *

After a quiet morning and lunch, Jane went back to their quarters to prepare for another lesson in yoga. De Silva was in the garden deliberating how to spend his afternoon when he saw Anzan coming in his direction.

'Bhante Gunananda asked me to find you, sahib,' said the young man when he reached him. 'He hopes you have time to visit him this afternoon.'

'All the time in the world,' said de Silva. 'My wife is busy, and I have no plans.'

As he made his way to Gunananda's quarters, he wondered why the monk wanted to see him. Did he know that he and Jane were soon leaving and wanted to wish them goodbye? Perhaps that was it. Thinking of leaving, his mind turned to Anzan. He had served them well as had Chatura and he must mention that to Soma and Gunananda, but it was still a mystery why, in contrast to Chatura, Anzan seemed unhappy. Would it be going beyond the bounds of propriety to draw that to their attention? If they would speak to Anzan and ask what the matter was, he might be relieved to have the opportunity to unburden himself.

By the time he arrived at Gunananda's door, de Silva was still undecided about whether he should mention his concern for Anzan and if so, when would be the best time to do it. He heard voices inside and paused. Obviously Gunananda wasn't alone. He knocked and a voice that sounded like Soma's invited him to come in. To his surprise, the atmosphere in the small room was very different from what it had been on his earlier visit. The feeling of serenity that had then pervaded the room was absent and both monks looked ill at ease.

'Is there some problem that you need my help with?' asked de Silva.

Soma nodded. 'I'm afraid so. The monk in charge of our manuscripts has reported that one has gone missing, presumably stolen, but I'll let Bhante Gunananda explain.'

De Silva waited for Gunananda to speak. The old monk looked much frailer than he had on their first meeting and seemed to be having difficulty framing his words. Sadly, de Silva remembered his father's declining years and how there had been good days and bad days.

'Shall I tell the story after all?' asked Soma gently when a few moments had elapsed.

Gunananda nodded.

'It begins nearly sixty years ago when a traveller arrived at the monastery. His name was Bartholomew Parry, and he came seeking a place where he could live in peace and recover his health. Bhante Gunananda was young at the time but remembers him well. Parry was a very scholarly man and spent a lot of his time reading and writing. Bhante Gunananda was given the task of serving him. Although he often seemed distressed by something, Parry was very kind.'

'I think it is not too much to say that he came to regard me as a friend and I him,' said Gunananda, finding his voice. 'He taught me many things. He even tried to teach me to read and write English, but I'm afraid I was not a very good student.' The old monk smiled but de Silva saw that his eyes were moist.

'He had been here a few months when he showed me a manuscript that he had brought with him. It was contained in a leather pouch and made of a material that was unfamiliar to me, something dry that crackled and crumbled a little when Parry unrolled it to show it to me. He said it was not made of paper but vellum, a material derived from the skin of a calf which had been cleaned, stretched, and scraped until it was smooth enough to be written on. The writing on this manuscript was the colour of autumn leaves. Parry said it would once have been black, but time had faded it. The date of the manuscript indicated that it was a little over twelve hundred years old.'

Gunananda's voice had become increasingly hoarse. He stopped speaking and tried to clear his throat.

'Shall I go on, Bhante?' asked Soma. Again, the old monk nodded.

'Parry told Bhante Gunananda that the manuscript was written in an ancient version of the Welsh language, Parry's native tongue. If it was as old as the date indicated, it came from a time when very few people knew how to read or write. Those who did would have been monks or scholars. The latter would have lived and worked in one of the great universities that already existed at the time or perhaps in the houses of noble, even royal, families.'

Gunananda recovered and took up the story once more. 'Parry was a Christian. When I was young, I knew nothing about what Christians believed, but he taught me many things, in particular the Christian belief in an almighty God whose son Jesus Christ was born of a virgin. He lived in a country called Judea and the authorities in those days hated and feared him as a challenge to their power. They persuaded their Roman overlords to have him killed but he rose again from the dead and ascended to Heaven.'

De Silva nodded. 'I know the story so far.'

'Then perhaps you also know that some of his followers, who came to be called Christians in his honour, had to flee persecution. Parry said that some of them went to Britain, landing in the west of the island in a place called Cornwall. He told me this happened hundreds of years before other Christians came from Rome and settled in the east of Britain, eventually driving the first settlers further west into the safety of the remote valleys and mountains of Wales where they built monasteries.'

'Perhaps that would be the reason why this manuscript you're talking about was written in Welsh,' suggested de Silva.

'Yes.'

Gunananda began to cough and motioned to Soma to go on.

'One part of the manuscript concerned Jesus's life between the ages of twelve and thirty. Parry explained to Bhante Gunananda that the Christians' holy books, which they call gospels, have nothing to say about those years, but legends and folklore in Wales and Cornwall mention a wealthy and influential man called Joseph of Arimathea who made his money by trading in metals found in the British Isles. Cornwall in particular was rich in tin, a prized metal in those days that was exported all over the known world. Mixed with copper it made bronze, which is stronger than both of them and was used for weapons.'

Soma paused and glanced at Gunananda, but the old monk didn't show any inclination to carry on with the story, so he continued. 'Parry also explained that since the gospels soon cease to mention Jesus's father Joseph, some people think it's possible that Joseph died when Jesus was still a child. The manuscript claimed this was true, as was the legend that Joseph of Arimathea was a close relation of Jesus and took Jesus into his care, bringing him to Britain on some of Joseph's voyages to the island.'

'It sounds plausible.'

'Apparently, before Christians came to Britain,' Soma went on, 'its people followed a religion led by priests called Druids. They were deeply spiritual and important men in their communities. Parry told Bhante Gunananda that the gospels describe Jesus as a remarkably intelligent and curious boy. He even dared to dispute with the religious elders in his own country. If he came to Britain, Parry asked, would he not have been eager to meet these Druids and learn about their beliefs?'

De Silva thought for a moment, digesting all the information he had heard. 'But how can one know if the manuscript tells the truth?'

'I agree it's impossible, but if it's as old as it purports to be, it adds weight to the legends Parry spoke of and would presumably be valuable simply on account of its great age.'

'I suppose that's true but if someone took it, what would they do with it?'

'I imagine they would hope to sell it.'

'There is more,' said Gunananda. 'It was clear to me, young as I was, that Parry was a very troubled man. I would often find him studying the manuscript. Sometimes he didn't speak for days and simply sat there, barely touching the food I brought to him. At other times he would walk for hours on the mountainside or in the forest, coming back with his feet blistered and bleeding, wounds he seemed not to notice. Eventually, he fell ill and despite all our efforts, we couldn't save him. In his last days, he suffered from a high fever and often became agitated. At those times he often spoke of another, more troubling and even older, story in the manuscript, a claim that Jesus's mother had also visited Britain with Joseph of Arimathea whilst she was betrothed to her future husband Joseph. When she returned to Judea to marry him, she was pregnant by a British nobleman. The child she bore was Jesus.'

'Do you mean the manuscript claims that Jesus's father was a mortal man?'

'Yes.'

De Silva took a moment to register the significance of all this. 'But why would a Christian repeat such a tale? Doesn't it deny one of their religion's central beliefs?'

'You make a very good point,' said Soma. 'Perhaps he was someone who had lost his faith, someone malicious or both.'

'When I cleared Parry's effects,' said Gunananda, 'I found his diaries amongst them. There were many entries about the manuscript. He was very torn about what to do with it. His illness may have affected his mind, but it seemed he feared it contained truth and had begun to doubt his faith.'

'Are you sure this manuscript has been stolen? Could it simply have been mislaid?'

'I'm afraid not,' said Soma. 'After Bartholomew Parry died, Bhante Gunananda asked Bhante Toshin who was then the most senior monk in the monastery what he should do with it. Bhante Toshin considered the matter carefully. He decided it was not for him to make the decision to destroy it and it was impossible to know whether Parry would ultimately have done so. On the other hand, he did not want to ignite what might be a very serious religious conflict. Accordingly, he ordered the manuscript to be put in a safe place in the room where we keep our own manuscripts. It adjoins the prayer hall.'

'Exactly where was this safe place?'

'A box in a locked cupboard.'

'Was there a lock on the box?'

'No.'

'What about the cupboard? Was the lock forced?'

'It seems to be intact.'

'So unless someone picked the lock, they knew where key was, or managed to find it.'

'We fear that whoever has taken the manuscript means to use it to do harm.'

'When did this monk first realise that it was missing?'

'Only this morning. He went to the cupboard to take out something else and noticed that the box had moved from its usual place.'

'Does he remember when he last saw it there?'

'I'll ask him,' said Soma.

'Do you trust him to say nothing about the theft for the moment?'

'I do.'

'Who else has access to the library?'

'It's never locked.' Soma looked embarrassed. 'Until now, there never seemed to be any need to do so. Of course things will have to change.'

'So anyone could enter from the prayer hall,' mused de Silva. 'Does a person who goes to the library regularly spring to mind? I mean other than the monk who is in charge. Alec Wragge, for example? I believe he's here to study your religious texts.'

Gunananda looked uncertain. 'Are you suggesting he's the thief?'

'I'm not accusing anyone, at least not yet.'

'So, you will help us to investigate the theft?' Soma's expression brightened. 'We'd be most grateful.' He turned to Gunananda, who murmured something unintelligible.

It might mean staying on longer than he and Jane had planned, thought de Silva. He wasn't due to go back to work immediately on their return to Nuala, so he had a bit of time on his side, but if that ceased to be the case, he would have to explain the delay to Archie. As the necessity might not arise, however, he decided not to mention it to Soma and Gunananda yet.

'I'll be glad to do anything in my power to help,' he said.

Soma pressed the palms of his hands together and gave a little bow. 'Thank you.' He got to his feet. 'I'm afraid I must leave you now. I have many things to attend to before prayers, and I expect Bhante Gunananda needs to rest.'

'Of course.'

'Shall we speak again tomorrow?'

De Silva nodded. 'Yes, and for the moment I suggest you carry on as if nothing has happened.'

* * *

'Have you been for another walk?' asked Jane when de Silva found her in their quarters. She put aside the book she had been reading and took off her glasses. 'I finished my yoga lesson a while ago.'

'No, I had an invitation to visit Bhante Gunananda, and something I certainly hadn't expected came up.'

Jane's expression became increasingly perplexed as he told her about the meeting and the monks' request for his help.

'I know that there are old tales about Joseph of Arimathea that claim he visited Britain, and that Jesus may have done so too,' she said when he had finished. 'Do you recall the hymn, 'Jerusalem'? We sing it sometimes in church. It begins, *and did those feet, in ancient times.*'

'Hmm, let me see, yes, vaguely. It's the one with the rousing tune, isn't it?'

'That's right.'

'Then if the hymn is sung in church, am I right in thinking that Christians recognise and accept the possibility that Jesus visited Britain?'

'Some do, although I doubt that the idea of Jesus studying with Druids would meet with approval. The Church looks on them as pagans. As for the suggestion that there's no truth in the biblical story of the Virgin birth, I'm absolutely certain that the Church would regard that as heresy, and as far as I'm concerned, it's nonsense, and shocking nonsense too.' Jane put her reading glasses in their case and closed it with a snap. 'This manuscript may be as old as it purports to be or it may be a later forgery, but clearly it was written by someone who just wanted to make trouble.'

De Silva rested a hand on her shoulder. 'I'm sorry, my love, I didn't mean to upset you.'

Jane rallied. 'I know you didn't, and none of this is your fault. I just hope any sensible person would see the story for the wicked lie it is.'

'All the same,' he said cautiously, 'it might be interesting to know more about the manuscript. If someone thought that it was worth stealing, it indicates it has considerable value, perhaps just on account of its age.'

'I suppose it might,' said Jane. 'Although I'm not sure how it would be possible to tell if it really dates from the seventh or eighth century,' she added.

'Perhaps not at the present, but I've read of experiments in America that involve something called radiocarbon dating. I expect it's much too early for it to be generally available, but it might be in the not-too-distant future.'

Jane raised an eyebrow. 'So we're looking for a thief with a great deal of patience, who understands a dead language, and somehow knew that a controversial manuscript was hidden in a remote monastery in Ceylon.'

'When you put it like that, it does sound rather preposterous, but stranger things have happened. This man Parry may have left letters or diaries other than the ones Gunananda saw that referred to the manuscript, or he may have mentioned it to someone else who subsequently wrote about it. People can be very persistent in their pursuit of money.'

'I give in,' said Jane, shaking her head. 'But I still refuse to believe the claim about Mary. It's nothing more than sacrilegious nonsense.'

'I won't argue with you about that, but I hope you agree that as the manuscript was left to the monastery, it ought to be found and kept here.'

Jane sighed. 'I suppose so, however abhorrent its contents are. And of course, one doesn't want the wrong kind of person getting hold of it. Do you think whoever took it has already left the monastery?'

'It's possible, but there are more questions that I'll need to ask Gunananda and Soma.' He looked at his watch. 'We'll be expected for dinner soon and afterwards the monks will be at prayer, so it will have to wait until tomorrow.'

'Oh dear, these things can go on so. Will we still be able to leave when we planned to? I have to admit, I'm starting to miss home.'

'I hope so, but one can never be sure. Soma and Gunananda were very pressing about needing my help. I don't want to let them down.'

'And I don't want the servants worried about what might have happened to us.'

'Neither do I. If we have to delay our departure, I ought to drive back to Nuala anyway to explain to Archie what's going on. I could fit in a visit to Sunnybank at the same time and reassure them. You could always come with me and then stay on at home. Would you rather do that?'

Jane thought for a moment. 'It would look suspicious if we both left and then you came back on your own.'

'Yes, I suppose it would. If it comes to it then, do you mind staying? We can say we've decided to extend our visit, but I just need to deal with a pressing matter that will take me away for a day.'

Jane gave him a rueful smile. 'Much as I love a mystery, I wish this one hadn't arisen, but I suppose it can't be ignored.'

'No, so let's hope finding the answer won't take too long. To be honest, I'm not sure if the monastery is within my jurisdiction anyway. I'd need to find that out. If not, I can just hand everything over to the appropriate police force.'

CHAPTER 7

De Silva and Jane had finished breakfast the following morning and were returning to their apartment when Anzan came to fetch him. De Silva wondered if the young monk knew what had happened. If he did, he gave no hint of it and was his usual subdued self. He led de Silva to a different building to the one where he had met Soma and Gunananda the previous evening, and showed de Silva in.

Soma came forward to greet him. 'Thank you for coming. Bhante Gunananda won't be joining us this morning. This business has caused him considerable distress and I suggested he spend the morning resting and meditating. I believe I should be able to answer any questions, but if not, I will speak with him later. Now, shall we sit down?'

De Silva was glad to see that there were two stools in the room. He lowered himself onto one of them and took out his notebook.

There was a knock and Soma called out to come in. A young monk de Silva didn't recognise appeared with two small bowls and a brass teapot. De Silva accepted some tea and waited for him to leave before he opened his notebook and asked Soma the first question.

'So, back to where we were yesterday. You were going to find out when the manuscript was last seen.'

'Yes, I spoke with the monk in charge of our library after prayers yesterday evening. He said he doesn't often go to the cupboard where Parry's manuscript was kept, but he did so about four weeks ago. He recalls that the box was in its usual place then, and everything looked normal.'

De Silva made a note. 'Then we can narrow the theft down to sometime over the last four weeks. Apart from the community, who has been at the monastery in that time?'

'Only the guests that you've met.'

'All of whom are still here now,' said de Silva, half to himself, and made another note. 'Have any of the monks not been at the monastery long?'

'Mostly just the young ones.'

'And amongst them?'

'Anzan, who serves you, has been here for the least time.'

'What do you know about him?'

'He comes from a village not far from here. He's a bright young man and his parents were very keen that he should enter the monastery.'

'So, is he doing well here?'

'Why do you ask?' Soma looked surprised. 'I hope he has served you and your wife to your satisfaction.'

'Yes, he has, but we've noticed that compared with Chatura, he's very quiet. It's as if something is troubling him.'

A furrow appeared between Soma's eyebrows. 'Are you suggesting that's evidence of guilt?'

'I never jump to conclusions, but at this stage everything needs to be considered. Are there many times when he or any of the other monks are alone?'

'It's very rare for that to be the case.'

'How about in the last four weeks?'

'I can't think of a particular occasion.'

Although Anzan was alone when I saw him tending the goats, thought de Silva. 'Can you think of anyone who's left the monastery over the same period?'

'As you will have noticed, the monks go out each

morning to collect alms, but otherwise no. I'm afraid that at the moment I really can't think of anything that might help. I'm sorry to be of so little use to you.'

De Silva sighed inwardly. It looked as if getting to the bottom of this mystery wasn't going to be straightforward. He studied Soma thoughtfully. His manner was now far less decisive than it had been the previous evening. Had he been the one who had wanted to involve the police, or had it really been Gunananda's idea? Was that the reason why Soma had arranged to see him alone this morning? Did he hope to close down the investigation for his own purposes? At this stage it was always unwise to discount anyone as a suspect. De Silva's mind went back to the couple he'd seen coming down the mountain at dawn. It was certainly a very odd time to be out there. If it was Soma and Madeleine, what had they been up to?

* * *

'Did you find out anything useful?' asked Jane when after a few more minutes' conversation with Soma, he came to find her sitting in the garden. She had finished the final chapter of her book and was filling in a crossword in the puzzle book she had brought with her.

'It was rather a strange interview,' said de Silva after he had told her the gist of his conversation with Soma. 'Yesterday he asked for my help, but today he seemed very short of suggestions for the direction I might take my investigations in. It was almost as if he would prefer to let the matter drop.'

'Maybe he really doesn't have any ideas, but I suppose there could be other reasons for his reticence. He may feel guilty that with all the other improvements he's made, he hasn't done more over the years to improve the security of the monastery's valuables.'

'I'm afraid that would be with good reason.'

'He might have called on you in the heat of the moment, and now wishes he hadn't. Perhaps he would always have preferred to keep the theft quiet and only acquiesced yesterday in order to please Bhante Gunananda. After all, Soma never met this man Bartholomew Parry, so may not feel the same burden of responsibility for keeping his manuscript safe that Gunananda presumably does. It may be that as far as Soma is concerned, the manuscript isn't of particular interest. It's just something that relates to a religion that he has no connection with.'

'Hmm, he seemed pretty eager to recover it yesterday, but you may have hit on something there.'

Jane raised an eyebrow. 'Thank you, dear.'

De Silva grinned. 'I meant no offence. Anyway, unfortunately the meeting hasn't got me any further forward.'

'Well, let's look at the possibilities. The first one being that the person who took the manuscript sneaked into the monastery from outside and managed to get into the library, then picked the lock of the cupboard or found the key, discovered the box, and removed the manuscript, all without being observed by anyone.'

'It does seem rather unlikely.'

'Yes, it does. They would need to be sure of what they were looking for and where it was likely to be. Also they probably wouldn't have much time, whereas someone who was already here would have had the chance to narrow down the places where the manuscript might be.'

'That's true,' said de Silva.

'Despite what Soma told you about no one leaving the monastery in the last four weeks, except for the monks on their expeditions for alms, I wouldn't rule out the possibility that the manuscript is no longer here.' Jane put a hand to her forehead. 'How could I forget? Soma left the monastery, didn't he? When he came to the vicarage.'

'He might have thought it irrelevant or forgotten.'

'Or hoped we would. Thinking about Soma's visit to Reverend Peters, it was an unusual step to take. It would have been easy for Soma to steal the manuscript sometime during the last four weeks and take it with him. When Reverend Peters invited us ladies to meet him, I understand the arrangement hadn't been long made. He could have stolen the manuscript before he contacted Reverend Peters or done so once he'd been in touch with him. Either way, it would have been a neat way of removing it from the monastery. How do we find out what else he did in Nuala or who else he visited?'

'That may be difficult. People are used to seeing monks about in the town, and their robes act as cloaks of anonymity.' De Silva rubbed his chin. 'I suppose I could ask Reverend Peters if Soma mentioned going anywhere else. If he has something to hide, however, I doubt he would be so careless as to give his movements away, but one never knows.' He paused. 'Going back to that couple I saw on the mountainside, if it was Soma and Madeleine, could there be a connection to the theft? Maybe the manuscript's still here and she's the person who's going to smuggle it out of the monastery.'

'I'd be surprised if she'd agree to take part in a crime for money when she's such a successful author.'

'Are you sure about that?'

'What do you mean?'

De Silva shrugged. 'She obviously likes to spend lavishly. Maybe the standard of living she likes to enjoy requires more money than she can earn.'

'Perhaps, but on the other hand, she may simply want to help Soma,' said Jane. 'Maybe they really are romantically involved, shocking as that sounds for a man who made a vow to renounce that kind of thing.' She stopped. 'What are you smiling at?'

'You, finding the romantic angle.'

Jane sniffed. 'You considered it too.'

De Silva laughed. 'I know, and we ought to keep it in mind. We also need to think about a motive. Looking back to our first evening here, what Arthur said about Soma is interesting.'

'Do you mean that he couldn't understand how Soma had found the money to restore the monastery?'

'Yes. On reflection, would the money paid by the guests who've stayed here and perhaps made some extra donations be enough? The work might easily have cost more. If Soma's guilty, it might account for his vagueness this morning. Whilst he was with Bhante Gunananda, he needed to keep up the pretence that he was as anxious as Gunananda to find the thief and recover the manuscript, but in reality, he knows exactly where it is and has no intention of returning it.'

'Do you think this wouldn't be the first time he's stolen something valuable from the monastery?'

'It's certainly something to consider. I'd like to look more into it as well as keeping a careful eye on anyone leaving from now on.'

'Yes.'

Jane was silent for a moment. A bee landed on a trumpet-shaped flower nearby and de Silva watched it disappear between the lilac petals until all that remained outside was its waggling brown bottom. He envied it that its quest for pollen was so much easier than the search he and Jane were embarking on. Already there was Soma to consider and perhaps Madeleine too. Then there was Alec Wragge. Could money be the motive there? Certainly, he was one of the people that they needed to look into.

'Or Alec might simply desire to possess something as old and rare as this manuscript might be,' said Jane when he mentioned Wragge's name. 'We haven't considered Arthur yet, have we? After all, he's left the monastery in the last four weeks like Soma. But he *is* a clergyman and doesn't seem to have any interests in old manuscripts.'

'Even clergymen can be interested in money.'

'And there was that evasiveness about his past life.' Jane rested her head on her hand and sighed. 'How quickly everything has changed.'

There was movement over by the entrance gate. Some of the monks were returning from the villages with their bowls of alms. Many of them were talking and laughing. De Silva imagined the dismay it would cause if they knew that he and Jane were entertaining the idea that Bhante Gunananda's respected deputy was a thief. Soma would not only have committed a crime, but he would have broken a vow that was central to the teaching they all believed in.

'I think it would be worth having a look at this library,' he said. 'As I've no equipment with me, I won't be able to take any fingerprints and no doubt whoever got into the cupboard would have wiped everything clean anyway, but the room may teach us something.'

'I'll come with you.'

De Silva looked at his watch; it was past midday 'We'd better wait until after lunch. We're already late and it might cause comment if we miss it.'

Arthur Warrender was in the dining room but there was no sign of Madeleine Moreton or the Wragges.

'Ah, good,' he said. 'I feared I would be eating alone today.' He winked and lowered his voice. 'I expect our fare will be the usual dahl, and it tastes so much better in good company.'

Jane smiled. 'Thank you.'

The table was set with bowls, glasses, and spoons, and soon Chatura arrived with a serving bowl containing dahl. 'I'll come back with the water,' he said.

'Is Anzan not here today?' asked Jane.

'Bhante Soma told him to mend the goats' shelter.'

'I understand that before he entered the monastery, Anzan worked with his father, who is a carpenter,' remarked Arthur when Chatura had left the room. 'An excellent skill to possess, carpentry, and one with a noble history. The bible tells us that Jesus's earthly father Joseph was a carpenter.'

They helped themselves to the dahl. De Silva was gratified to find that it was tastier than usual and contained a few chopped vegetables and herbs, presumably from the monastery garden.

'I may not be having many more meals of this,' said Arthur as they ate. 'I'm thinking of leaving quite soon. What about you?'

'We'd also planned to go home shortly, but we were just saying that it's so beautiful up here that we may stay on a little longer,' replied Jane. 'Shanti left his sergeant in charge of the police station in Nuala and he's a very capable young man.'

Arthur smiled. 'It sounds like you're lucky to have him.'

'Indeed I am.' De Silva chuckled. 'Another year or two and he'll probably be taking over my job.'

'Surely not.'

'Oh, it wouldn't be such a bad thing. We all have to retire one day. I'll be happy to do so if I know I'm leaving Nuala in safe hands.'

'I've certainly found retirement most congenial.'

'Have you made good progress with your writing whilst you've been here?' asked Jane.

'I'm delighted to say that I have.' Arthur smiled ruefully. 'Whether the fruits of my labours will ever see the light of day is another matter.'

'Oh, I'm sure they will. Plants are such a popular subject.'

'You're very kind. In any case, the project keeps me occupied. Writing and research take up a great deal of my time, and when one is alone in life, that is something to be grateful for. Madeleine says much the same. Although we labour in very different fields, we often talk about our work. She possesses a more serious turn of mind than her outward appearance indicates.'

De Silva's ears pricked up. Had Madeleine gone out of her way to give that impression to a man who might otherwise wonder why she wanted to spend so long away from the wider world?

'But as for Alec Wragge,' Arthur went on, 'I've really no idea exactly what his work entails. He's a difficult man to talk to.' He turned to Jane and lowered his voice. 'I hope I can rely on you not to repeat this, but as my rooms are next to theirs and the walls are paper thin, I'm often disturbed by their arguments.'

'I'm afraid that all couples argue sometimes,' said Jane. 'But it's very sad if they argue a lot. The Wragges seem so young too. She can't be more than twenty-five and he not much older. Do you know if they've been married for long?'

'Belinda once mentioned that they honeymooned in Galle just after the war.'

'Not long then.'

'Anyway, I may not be disturbed by them for much longer. As I was getting ready to come to lunch, I heard them arguing again, and there was something about leaving for Colombo very soon. It surprised me as I thought the university where Alec teaches had given him a considerable amount of time off, enabling them to stay here for several more weeks.' He shrugged. 'I must have misunderstood.'

Arthur changed the subject and de Silva's attention drifted from the conversation. Perhaps when the Wragges were not constantly thrown into each other's company, he thought, it would be easier for them to get on, but their marital difficulties were of no particular interest to him. It was thought-provoking, however, that they might be leaving sooner than expected, especially since Alec was often in the library and his field of study was ancient religious manuscripts. He and Jane would have to decide what to do about the Wragges.

He was still considering that when he noticed that Arthur was on his feet.

'Forgive me if I leave you now. There's a great deal I'd like to do this afternoon. I look forward to continuing our chat at dinner.'

'That was interesting,' said Jane when the door had closed behind him.

'The fact that the Wragges may be leaving?'

'Not only that, but what Arthur overheard them saying in one of their arguments a few nights ago.'

'Oh, what was that?'

'Shanti! You should have been listening.'

'I was most of the time,' grumbled de Silva, 'but I didn't think he had anything more to say about the Wragges.'

'He went back to the subject.'

'Ah, then tell me what I missed.'

'Arthur heard Belinda beg her husband not to do the wrong thing. Apparently, she sounded very agitated. He thought it might be something to do with their marriage or perhaps his work, because Belinda said something about manuscripts.'

'Hmm, but it might have been something to do with our missing manuscript.'

'Yes, it might.'

* * *

Lunch over, they walked to the prayer hall and went inside. It was pleasantly cool, providing a welcome change from the heat outside. None of the lamps were lit but the light that filtered through the entrance doors picked out the shrine where, with serene face and downcast eyes, the statue of the seated Buddha sat in silent contemplation. Thick woven carpets muffled their footsteps as they crossed the hall and entered the room where the monastery's books and manuscripts were kept. It was spacious with a high ceiling and walls lined with shelving. De Silva noticed the rich smell of well-aged wood.

The librarian looked up from the book he was studying and greeted them. 'Bhante Soma said you would want to speak with me.' He rose and, placing the palms of his hands together, dipped forward in a bow. Jane and de Silva followed his example. He indicated the shelves. 'This is where we keep our books and manuscripts. Most of them are of considerable antiquity and consequently very fragile. They must be treated extremely carefully to prevent them from being damaged.'

Jane and de Silva looked at the book he had been studying when they came in. 'How beautiful it is,' said Jane. Lines of elegant calligraphy bordered a jewel-coloured painting of the seated Buddha preaching to a smiling devotee wearing a saffron robe. Lotus flowers bloomed in the background and the image was framed by a cinquefoil arch decorated with delicate gold filigree. Across the bottom of the page cavorted a multitude of tiny creatures, some fantastical and some human in form. The effect was so vibrant that de Silva half expected the characters to leap off the page before his very eyes. It really was astonishing that such an exquisite object and others like it had not been kept under lock and key, and even more so that Soma, who seemed more familiar with the ways of the world than Bhante Gunananda, had let the state of affairs continue.

For a moment, the librarian too gazed at the picture before rousing himself. 'You've come to ask about Bartholomew Parry's manuscript. I will show you where it was kept.'

Reverently, he wrapped up the illuminated book in a thick cloth, returned it to its place on the shelves and went over to a cupboard. He took a key from a nearby drawer, opened the cupboard and pointed to the box inside. 'The manuscript was stored in a pouch in there.'

He lifted the box out and gave it to de Silva. The wood was thin. Even if the box had been locked, de Silva thought, it wouldn't have been hard to break into it, but then the theft would have been more immediately obvious.

'Do many of the monks use the library?' he asked.

'Some of them when they wish to study.'

'Would that only be in the daytime?'

'I believe so. It's dark here after sunset. In any case when evening prayers are over, it's our time for meditation, and as we rise before dawn each day, we go early to bed.'

'And are you here all day?'

'Unless I am called away by Bhante Gunananda or Bhante Soma, or it is time for the midday meal.'

'I understand all the monks eat together.'

'Yes.'

De Silva looked around him. 'You have many books here, perhaps not as fine as the one you just showed us, but they must be valuable. Why was the library never locked?'

The librarian shook his head sadly. 'Bhante Soma never ordered it as it didn't seem necessary.'

De Silva and Jane exchanged glances.

'But from now on,' continued the monk, 'he has ordered that a watch be kept day and night.'

'Have any of the guests at the monastery visited the library in the last few weeks?'

'Only Alec Wragge. He comes here to write and study.'

'Has he ever asked about Bartholomew Parry?'

'No, he only seems interested in our Buddhist texts.'

'Does he ever talk to you about his work?'

'Occasionally, but I think he prefers to avoid

conversations.' A worried expression came over the librarian's face. 'Do you think you will find this manuscript? Bhante Gunananda is very concerned about its loss. He knew Bartholomew Parry and had profound respect for him.'

'I don't know,' said de Silva, 'but I'll certainly do my best.'

The librarian smiled. 'Bhante Soma says that you are a famous detective.'

'He's very kind.'

'Is there anything else you would like to see?'

'I think that's all, thank you.'

The librarian replaced the box in the cupboard and locked it again. As he stepped away, de Silva noticed a small wooden stepladder in the nearby corner. Some of the treads looked much newer than others.

'What do you use that for?' he asked.

'We have a few high cupboards that cannot be reached from the ground.'

De Silva bent down and inspected the steps. 'It looks like someone has done a good job of repairing it. Was it done recently?'

The librarian nodded. 'About ten days ago. Two of the steps were dangerous. One of our young monks is skilled in carpentry so Bhante Soma told him to see what could be done. The wood had warped and cracked so he replaced it.'

'Would that be Anzan?'

'Yes.' The librarian looked a little surprised.

'Along with Chatura, he's looking after us. I understand he usually carries out any carpentry that needs doing around the monastery. Well, thank you for your help. We'll leave you to get on with your work.'

They exchanged farewells, and de Silva and Jane went through the hall and back into the sunshine.

'That was interesting,' said Jane. 'I mean what the librarian said about Anzan mending the stepladder.'

'Yes, it suggests he'd have the tools to pick a lock if he wanted to, but the key to that cupboard was hardly difficult to find. I fear we must definitely add him to our list of suspects. I didn't want to ask too many questions in case the librarian became suspicious, so we don't know how closely he supervised Anzan. If he left him to get on with the work alone, Anzan would have had time to get into that cupboard and take the manuscript.'

'But why look in there at all?'

'Possibly because he thought that a locked cupboard would contain something valuable.'

'Yes, but why take this particular manuscript? What would make him think it was worthwhile?'

De Silva shrugged. 'I can't answer that for the moment.'

'He would need to conceal it somehow to remove it from the library.'

'That wouldn't be too hard. Carpenters usually carry their tools in a roomy bag.'

'But if Anzan's just a simple monk, how would he know how to sell a valuable manuscript?'

'He probably wouldn't, but he might have taken it for someone else. His task would be to steal it and smuggle it out of the monastery. It may be that our arrival interrupted the plan. As he'd been told by Soma to look after us, it would be much harder for him to leave the monastery to meet that someone.'

'Then we may be wrong in thinking he's unhappy. The emotion we've noticed may be guilt or fear of being found out.' Jane sighed. 'I hate to think that he's the thief. He still reminds me so much of Prasanna that it's hard to believe he's done anything wrong.'

'One should never go by appearances.'

'I know. Well, if he took the manuscript, we're left with the question of what he's done with it if he hasn't had time to smuggle it out. Surely it would be very difficult to hide it in the monks' quarters. They have very few possessions or places to keep them.'

De Silva thought for a moment. 'I'll tell you the most obvious place. The shed where the goats are kept. He could hide it there until we've gone, and he has the chance to meet whoever wants the manuscript. He could probably slip away unnoticed for a little while on one of those early morning trips to ask for alms.'

Jane considered the idea. 'That might be harder than you think, but if he is in league with someone, they could come when he's looking after the goats. They may already have done so.'

'Or they may not have. Those goats could be the key to solving our mystery. I think it's time I took a good look at their shed. If I find nothing, we can decide then what to do next.'

'Shall I come with you?'

'Best if you to stay here. One of us needs to try to keep an eye on Madeleine and Soma. It will be harder to watch Soma, but it shouldn't be too difficult to watch her.'

'Very well, I'll sit in the garden. There's a good view of the guest quarters from there so if she leaves, I'll notice. If she does, I'll try to follow her.' Jane paused for a moment. 'I ought to look as if I'm just relaxing but I've nothing left to read.'

'What about your crossword book?'

'Good thinking, that will do very well. Just wait a moment whilst I fetch it.'

'Don't get too immersed though, or you might miss something.'

'Don't worry, I won't.'

'I'll wait for you in the garden.'

Whilst he waited, de Silva made a show of inspecting the rows of vegetables the monks were growing. The glossy purple aubergines and scarlet tomatoes looked healthy but not as large as the ones he had left in their gardener Anif's care at Sunnybank. The earth up here was presumably thinner and less fertile than it was at the lower altitude, and he had discovered over the course of their stay that the nights were cooler.

The latch on the garden gate clicked, and Jane reappeared with the crossword book in her hand. She had put on her straw hat and a pair of sunglasses. 'Now no one will know that I'm spying on Madeleine.'

'And a very elegant spy you make,' said de Silva with a grin. 'Right, I'll be off then.'

* * *

He left the main courtyard and headed out to look for Anzan. The way to where he had last seen him minding the goats lay through a grove of palm trees that provided welcome shade from the hot afternoon sun. He thought he heard the sound of bleating ahead but when he emerged into the clearing, he found there was no sign of the young monk or the goats. Perhaps Anzan had taken them somewhere else to find fresh grazing. He decided to take a quick look in the shed before he made a wider search.

It was very dark in the stuffy shed and the smell made his nostrils prickle. He saw movement at the far end and guessed that the goats were there after all. If he was to make any kind of search he would need to keep the door open to give himself some light, and he didn't want them to escape. Spotting a bale of hay nearby, he reached for its string. The coarse hemp chafed his palm, but he managed to pull the bale across so that it blocked the lower part of the entrance. Hopefully that would do the trick, at least for a while.

As his eyes became accustomed to the gloom, he made out six goats. Five seemed untroubled by his arrival, but the sixth, which sported a luxuriant pointed beard and had disturbingly large horns, stood and watched him with baleful eyes, its jaws slowly moving as it chewed the wisps of hay that straggled from its mouth. De Silva guessed he was the billy goat, and hoped he was too hot to take the trouble to defend his harem. He glanced around the rest of the shed. He wasn't entirely sure what he was looking for, but he had a hunch there might be something that would provide a clue as to what Anzan was up to.

A large, circular metal bin stood in one corner. The lid rattled as he lifted it off and found a yellow grain of some kind that gave off a sweetish smell; he guessed it was maize. Rolling up his sleeves, he plunged in one arm and felt around, the grains shifting and sliding between his fingers, but there was nothing unexpected there. He replaced the lid and turned his attention to a pile of hay bales that were stacked against a wall, but when he pulled them forward and peered down into the dark gap, he found nothing hidden.

Next, he noticed a tangled hay net with some old sacking under it. He pushed the net aside and picked up the top sack. Inside was a saffron robe, but before he could pull it out, there was a sound behind him. He felt a sharp nudge and turned to see the billy goat a few feet away from him, its head lowered. De Silva flapped his hands, and it retreated a little way, one hoof pawing at the hard ground, but then the harem started to bleat, and it advanced once more. Stepping back, de Silva shouted as he stumbled over the pile of sacking. The goat gave an angry snort and the other goats bleated even louder than before. With agility born of desperation, de Silva hauled himself back on his feet, barged past the indignant animal and made a dash for the open door. He vaulted the hay bale he had left as a barrier and, panting for breath, bent himself double with his palms on his knees. As his heartbeat returned to normal, he saw a movement in the periphery of his vision. He straightened up and saw Anzan running into the grove of palm trees.

'Wait!' he shouted, but Anzan kept running. Reluctantly, de Silva ran after him.

When he caught up, Anzan was slumped on the ground, the roughly ridged trunk of a palm tree supporting his back; instead of his robe, he wore everyday clothes. It was just as well he had stopped running, thought de Silva. Another trait the young monk shared with Sergeant Prasanna was fleetness of foot.

Anzan raised his head to meet de Silva's eyes. De Silva studied his expression and saw defiance and misery fighting for dominance. He folded his arms across his chest. 'I think you had better tell me what this is all about, young man.'

* * *

From where she sat in the garden, Jane kept one eye on the door to the guest apartments and the other on the crossword she was doing. She wondered how Shanti was getting on with Anzan. He seemed to have been gone a long time. Perhaps he'd not been able to find him.

She returned to her crossword and read the next clue. *What singer does with the French solo*. The answer must be *single* she decided. As she pencilled it in, she heard a door open, and glancing up, saw Madeleine Moreton emerge from the guest apartments. She spotted Jane and waved then started to walk over to the garden. Today she was resplendent in orange palazzo pants with a matching top. A black sunhat, gold sandals and a pair of outsized sunglasses with orange frames completed the outfit.

'Jane! What a pleasure to see you.' Madeleine sat down in one of the other chairs and looked at the book Jane was holding. 'I adore crosswords! I hope you haven't solved all of the clues already.'

'Nearly I'm afraid, but I've one to go back to that I'm stuck on. I blame it on the heat!'

Madeleine laughed. 'Always a handy scapegoat.' She took the book. '*Celebrate one being included in list of potential players*. Let me see… How about *roister*?'

'Oh well done, thank you.'

Jane closed the book and laid it down on the table beside her chair. 'Are you making good progress with your novel?'

'Tolerable. As usual, one comes to a point where the writing seems to go very slowly. Still, I've always found life here conducive to concentration.'

'Yes, there are far fewer distractions than in the outside world. Shanti and I have found it very restful.'

'Of course where there are people there are always some distractions,' remarked Madeleine.

'And I suppose that being a writer, you're drawn to observing how people behave and what they talk about.'

'I must admit, it's a habit one falls into, and it becomes hard to break.'

'Surely that's not a bad thing?'

'I hope not, as long as it doesn't divert one from the project in hand. The young monk who serves us at dinner sometimes, for example.'

'Chatura?'

'I don't think that's his name. I mean the other one.'

'Anzan?'

'Yes, he's the one. Don't you think he always looks unhappy? I wonder if he's in some kind of trouble. I've noticed he frequently goes off by himself.'

Jane's antennae stirred. 'I have noticed he seems rather subdued compared with Chatura, but perhaps he's just a quieter character. As for going off by himself, I believe he's often in charge of the monastery's little herd of goats.'

Madeleine laughed and patted Jane's arm. 'There you see, you have a sensible explanation for everything, whereas my imagination runs riot. It's the penalty of being a novelist. I can't help but weave a story around anyone who intrigues me. Poor Anzan, I'd already bestowed on him a terrible secret that he'd stop at nothing to protect.'

She adjusted her sunglasses. 'I expect you're right. He was probably just tending to the goats as you say. I really must stop daydreaming and concentrate on the story that I have in hand.'

She rose gracefully to her feet. 'Now, I must leave you. I came out with the intention of spending an hour or two in the prayer hall. I find its atmosphere so calming when I need to find a way to avoid a plot hole.'

'I'm sure the answer will come to you as quickly as the solution to my crossword clue did,' said Jane brightly.

'I hope you're right. I don't have much time left to find it. I need to leave here soon to attend to pressing commitments elsewhere.'

Madeleine's hand was on the metal ring that lifted the garden gate's latch when she turned back to look at Jane once more. 'Of course,' she said casually, 'having a vivid imagination doesn't necessarily prove one's wrong about something.'

The gate closed behind her, and Jane watched her glide away to the hall, her orange palazzo pants rippling as she walked. She climbed the broad steps and disappeared into the shadows. It hadn't been a casual encounter, Jane felt sure. She had the impression that Madeleine was very far from being whimsical and prone to daydreaming. There had been a purpose behind her conversation. Did she know that they had their suspicions about Anzan? Had she hoped to reinforce them, or if they weren't already there, plant them in their minds? Whatever the case, why would she want to do so unless it had something to do with whatever she and Soma might be hiding?

* * *

'I was beginning to think you were never coming back,' said Jane when de Silva re-joined her. 'Did you manage to find Anzan?'

'Yes, he wasn't with the goats when I got there, but he turned up in the end. In the meantime, I had to fend off an attack by an enraged billy goat that was determined to protect his harem at all costs. I was lucky to escape unscathed.' He gave her a detailed account of the incident with the billy goat, and Jane listened with amusement.

'I think you're taking the danger that I was in rather lightly,' he grumbled when he came to the end of the story.

Jane reached out and patted his arm. 'Only because you're safely back. I know that goats can be very troublesome, especially billy goats. I remember when the vicar's wife took a fancy to keeping a pair of goats. The vicarage's gardener eventually refused to go anywhere near the billy. Now, back to Anzan. I do so hope he had nothing to do with the theft.'

'You can rest easy, he didn't. Although at one point I was almost sure he was guilty. I discovered his robe hidden in the goats' shed, and when he came back and found me there, he was wearing ordinary clothes. He ran off at the sight of me, but I caught up with him. By then he didn't have much option but to tell me the whole story.'

He paused. Two monks were sweeping the courtyard and had come close to where they sat. Their desultory conversation was audible despite the swishing of their brooms. It would never do for them to overhear what he was about to say, so he waited until they were further away before he continued. 'You've said on more than one occasion that Anzan reminds you of Sergeant Prasanna, haven't you? Well, the similarity is more than skin deep. Poor Anzan is suffering from tribulations in love as Prasanna once did.'

'Oh dear, that *is* awkward.'

'Precisely. The girl comes from a village close to the one where he grew up and where his family still lives. He had hoped they and the girl's family would give their blessing to a marriage, but Anzan's father and mother wanted him to become a monk. There is, of course, considerable prestige involved for the family. They were convinced that what Anzan and this girl felt for each other was nothing more than a youthful infatuation that would soon pass.'

'Do I take it that it hasn't?'

'Yes. So, Anzan is torn between wanting to be with his girl and his duty to his parents. When I found him, he had just come back from a clandestine meeting with her.'

'What advice did you give him?'

'I suggested he speak with Bhante Gunananda. I believe that he's a good man and will be understanding. I'm sure he knows from his own experience that following the rule demands great dedication and sacrifice and is not for everyone.'

'But what about Anzan's parents?'

'Naturally, he will have to face them. They're likely to be very disappointed but hopefully they'll see reason in the end.'

'What if they don't, and refuse to have anything to do with him?'

'Anzan thinks they genuinely believed that entering the monastery was the best thing for him, but if they can be made to understand how strong his feelings are, they may relent, so although one can't rule out a rejection, the possibility seems remote. As a last resort, however, he has his skill as a carpenter and would be capable of making a living for himself and his girl, perhaps in one of the towns.'

'So what happens now?'

'Understandably, Anzan is nervous of approaching Bhante Gunananda on his own. I've offered to go with him and try to smooth the path.'

Jane smiled. 'It sounds like you have everything under control.'

'I certainly hope so, but sadly it brings us no closer to solving the mystery of who took this manuscript and what they've done with it. And the moment for doing that may already have passed.'

'Don't be too despondent. Whilst you were away, I had an interesting experience that may help us a little. I was here in the garden doing my crossword and keeping a look out for Madeleine or Soma, as we agreed, when Madeleine emerged from the guest quarters. There wasn't much danger of my not noticing her. She was wearing a very colourful outfit. Anyway, she came over to talk to me and was very friendly and chatty. She helped me with the crossword, and we talked a little about her writing, but she was up to something, I'm sure of it. She brought up the subject of Anzan looking miserable. She said she wondered if he was in some kind of trouble. She'd noticed he frequently went off on his own. I said I knew he was often in charge of the goats so that was probably where he went to, and as to the unhappiness, perhaps it was more the case that he was quieter than the other young monks.'

'How did she react to that?'

'Oh, she was very good humoured. She said something about letting her imagination run away with her and putting it down to being a novelist.'

'That's interesting.'

'I'm glad you agree. Perhaps she had an inkling that we suspected Anzan and wanted to fan the flames, or she didn't but hoped she could make us suspicious, with the aim of distracting attention from her and Soma and pointing us in the wrong direction.'

De Silva thought for a moment. 'I may even have put the idea into their heads. I remember that the first time Gunananda and Soma told me about the theft, we spoke of Anzan.'

'Why?'

'Only because I asked who had been at the monastery for the shortest time. They said it was Anzan and Soma asked if I suspected him. I said I suspected no one yet and the conversation moved on. If Soma is as clever as we think he is, however, he may have recalled my question and he and Madeleine are trying to nurture a seed that might already be in my mind.'

'So although Anzan would be exonerated eventually, in the meantime, Soma and Madeleine would have time to carry out whatever plan they have for the manuscript.'

'Did Madeleine mention that she would be leaving the monastery in the near future?'

Jane nodded. 'She claimed pressing commitments elsewhere.'

'Then we may not have much time.' He frowned. 'If Anzan and I speak to Gunananda immediately, it may cause some difficulty. It would be natural for Gunananda to pass on to Soma that we've ruled Anzan out of our investigation. If Soma and Madeleine are up to something, that may put them more on their guard.'

'Especially if Madeleine really was trying to cast suspicion on Anzan.'

'We don't have any solid evidence against Soma or Madeleine at present, so in my view it's too soon to tell Gunananda that we believe they may be the thieves.'

'If and when we do tell him, how do you think Gunananda will react?'

'Hard to say. He obviously relies on Soma so I doubt he'd want to believe ill of him, but I also trust he wouldn't think that I was making an accusation lightly.'

'What about Anzan?'

'At this stage, we can hardly let on to him that we think one of his superiors is a criminal.' He steepled his hands and rested his forehead on the tips of his fingers whilst he thought what to do.

'I feel rather guilty about keeping the poor lad waiting,' he said when he looked up again. 'Especially as when I offered to help him, he was touchingly grateful. But we need more time. I think I'll tell him that I've decided it's best if I approach Gunananda on my own first. As he previously believed that his situation was hopeless, now that there's some prospect of a happy ending, perhaps a few more days will be more bearable for him.'

'If Madeleine's leaving soon, it shouldn't be long before she and Soma make their move.'

De Silva shrugged. 'Unless they already have. In which case, our only option is to confront them, and I don't have much confidence in a good result to that.'

Jane stood up and stretched. 'I must take a short walk. I've been sitting for far too long.' She paused. 'Even if we do manage to keep an eye on Soma and Madeleine during the day, we still need to think about what to do during the night. If I were them, I'd prefer to meet once it's dark, so although dinner time and prayer time shouldn't be a problem, what about after that?'

De Silva thought about the layout of the guest quarters. The doors to the guests' rooms led off a verandah. His and Jane's door was situated on the right of the steps up to it with Madeleine's door beyond it. Arthur's door was on the left-hand side with Alec and Belinda Wragge's beyond. He was confident that if Madeleine went out in the night, she would go by the front. The bedroom windows at the rear of the building looked out over a steep slope covered in rough bushes that would be extremely difficult to negotiate.

'I'll sleep in the living room,' he said. 'It's nearest to the front door and if Madeleine goes out at night, it will give me the best chance of hearing her.'

'But won't you be terribly uncomfortable?'

'Not at all. I'll pull two chairs together and take a blanket and a pillow from the bedroom.'

'Why don't I take turns with you?'

'There's really no need.'

'Let's see. You may think differently after the first night.'

CHAPTER 8

An hour before prayer time, as de Silva and Jane were getting ready for dinner, Chatura knocked on the door of their apartment with a message from Soma.

'Soma wants to see me. I wonder what about,' said de Silva when he went into the bedroom to tell Jane.

'He may want to ask what progress you're making, which would be perfectly normal.'

'Yes, but in the circumstances, I'll have to be very careful what I say.'

'I wonder if Gunananda will be with him.'

'Hmm, I'm not sure if that would make the interview easier or harder.'

As he followed Chatura across the courtyard, the sun was already low in the sky, casting long shadows over the dusty ground. However many times it was swept, de Silva reflected, it would never be long before dust returned. Only when the monsoon rains came would that change, and then life at the monastery must be even harder than it was now. He pictured the monks, who usually went barefooted, squelching through sticky mud as they went about their work and devotions, and once again thought that theirs wasn't a life with which he would be content.

But in the warm evening light, there was no denying that the monastery buildings and their rocky setting were beautiful. The whitewashed walls and mellow clay tiles blended so well with their surroundings that it was almost as if they had grown naturally from the rocks, but of course that wasn't the case. A lot of work and materials must have gone into building them. Had donations and the income from a few guests really provided enough money to achieve the result he was looking at? Were he and Jane on the right track in thinking that there was a guilty secret behind Soma's success?

He and Chatura had almost reached Soma's door when a lad dressed in everyday clothes with a canvas satchel over his shoulder passed them. He greeted Chatura with a smile and Chatura smiled back.

'Who was that?' asked de Silva as they walked on.

'He comes up here from time to time if there are any letters to bring for Bhante Soma or the guests, stays a while and then goes back with any messages or replies that are needed.'

Perhaps he had brought a letter for the Wragges, thought de Silva, but had it really summoned them back to Colombo or was that a convenient fiction? He debated whether he should ask Chatura to find out if there had been a letter but decided against it. Maybe he would have the opportunity to talk privately to the postboy later.

Chatura left de Silva at Soma's door. When de Silva went in, he found the monk alone. His eyes were shrewd and watchful. De Silva wondered what was going on behind them. He reminded himself to be careful.

'Thank you for coming,' said Soma. 'I don't want to hurry you, but I'd be interested to know if you've found out anything of importance yet.'

'I'm afraid nothing so far, but it's still early days. I spoke to your librarian, and he showed me the place where the manuscript was kept. He also showed me some of your other treasures and I understand that you intend to improve their security.'

Soma looked irritated and de Silva silently congratulated himself. No doubt the monk saw himself as responsible for practical arrangements in the monastery, or the lack of them. If he could be wrong-footed, it might lead him to be less careful in what he said and to give something away that he otherwise would not have done.

'Between ourselves, I'm very concerned about Bhante Gunananda,' Soma went on. 'All this has distressed him greatly. It's clearly stirred up very painful memories of his friend Parry. It has even occurred to me that it might be best to abandon the search for the manuscript. Rather than the uncertainty as to whether the thief can be found, acceptance of the situation might enable Bhante Gunananda to be easier in his mind. After all, he's lived for many years by the teaching of the Buddha that we must renounce all attachment to worldly things if we are to attain wisdom and peace.'

De Silva noticed an expression that he couldn't quite read flit across Soma's face.

'I wouldn't advise giving up so soon. Most investigations take time, and I believe a crime shouldn't be overlooked unless there's truly no prospect of solving it. And it has to be borne in mind that even with better security, this theft may not be the last. What if there are more to come?'

'You have a point,' said Soma, but to de Silva his tone was distinctly reluctant. 'Very well, I'll accept your advice, but you will tell me if there's any progress, won't you?'

'Naturally,' said de Silva, adding to himself that it would depend in what direction that progress was leading.

The sound of a bell ringing drifted in from outside and Soma stood up. 'It's almost time for prayers.' He gave de Silva a perfunctory smile. 'Thank you for coming, I'm afraid I may have made you late for dinner.'

* * *

As de Silva emerged into the courtyard, some of the monks were already going up the steps to the prayer hall. The sun had nearly set, and the sky was streaked with rose and gold. In the distance, a flock of birds going to their roosts made a lazy curve across the sky. The scene had every appearance of a normal evening, but his mind was racing. Was Soma planning to use Bhante Gunananda's sorrow, which was no doubt genuine, as a way of concealing his crime?

Jane was at the door of their apartment to meet him. 'I didn't want to go to dinner without you,' she said. 'We'll just say it was me who made us late. No one will ask questions then. Tell me quickly how you got on.'

'As we anticipated, he asked if I'd made any progress. I told him not yet, that these things take time.'

'What did he have to say to that?'

'That was where it got interesting. He claims Bhante Gunananda is becoming very distressed, and it's even occurred to him, Soma I mean, that it might be best to give up the investigation and hope that Gunananda will find it easier to cope with the loss that way. He mentioned the Buddhist philosophy that acceptance is the path to wisdom and peace.'

'That certainly is interesting. I wonder if he'll bring up the idea again. If he's the thief, with or without Madeleine's help, it would be very convenient for him if you agreed.'

'It certainly would. All the more reason not to do so.'

'We ought to go to dinner now. We can talk more about this afterwards.'

* * *

The rest of the guests were already eating. Arthur Warrender's chair scraped on the stone-flagged floor as he stood up to greet them, but Alec Wragge remained seated, a moody expression on his face. Belinda Wragge gave them a tremulous smile.

Madeleine, who had changed from her orange palazzo pants into a black linen dress accessorised with a heavy gold necklace, made an expansive gesture in the direction of the large earthenware bowl in the middle of the table. 'Dahl again, I'm afraid, but there's plenty of it.' She patted the chair next to hers. 'Do come and sit here, Jane.' The other empty chair was to one side of Alec Wragge's. Madeleine raised an eyebrow. 'Alec dear,' she said pointedly. 'If you persist in sitting in that hunched up way with your elbows stuck out, poor Shanti will have great difficulty fitting into his seat.'

Alec flung her a hostile look, but he straightened his back and brought his elbows closer to his sides. 'Is that better?' he asked sourly.

Madeleine gave him a sweet smile that de Silva suspected was intended, with apparent success, to add to his irritation. Belinda's cheeks turned pink.

'It's my fault we're late,' said Jane.

'Your company is always worth waiting for,' Arthur said gallantly. De Silva thought he detected a flash of wry amusement in Madeleine's eyes.

'I was just saying how beautiful the sunrise was this morning,' Arthur went on. 'I always wake early. The penalty of advancing age I'm afraid.' He smiled at Alec and Belinda. 'Young people like you need to appreciate the blessings of youth before it's too late.'

Alec Wragge grunted, and Belinda's cheeks turned a deeper shade of pink.

'I believe Chatura and Anzan have gone to join in prayers now,' continued Arthur, ignoring Alec's snub. 'May I help you to some dahl?'

'No need,' said Jane. 'We can serve ourselves. Would you pass me those two bowls, Shanti?'

When Jane had filled the bowls, she and de Silva began to eat. The dahl had cooled, and briefly de Silva thought of the spread he might have been looking forward to at Sunnybank as he drank his pre-prandial whisky on the verandah with Bella on his lap. He liked dahl but more so when it was piping hot and accompanied by a variety of other dishes.

Jane, Arthur, and Madeleine were keeping up the conversation, so as he ate he had time to observe Alec and Belinda. When the other three tried to include them, Belinda's replies were short and delivered in a discomfited tone. She ate with an air of caution as if the dahl might turn to ashes in her mouth. Alec said not a word. De Silva was reminded that even though Soma was now their prime suspect, possibly in league with Madeleine, he ought not to discount the Wragges just yet.

'I hope you're not sickening for something, Alec,' said Madeleine when the conversation flagged, and his silence became oppressive.

'So what if I am?'

Belinda flinched and gave him an imploring look to which he paid no attention.

'Manners, old chap,' Arthur said pointedly. Alec mumbled an apology and Madeleine favoured him with another of her charming smiles.

'The fact is,' said Belinda quickly, 'we've had news from home. We have to leave much sooner than we expected.' De Silva paid attention. 'It's disappointing for Alec not to be able to complete his work here,' she added.

'Oh dear, what a shame,' said Madeleine. 'I know how frustrating it is when something gets in the way of one's work. Perhaps you'll be able to come back another time.'

'That's unlikely,' Alec muttered gruffly.

'We'll miss this place, won't we, dear,' said Belinda. 'And of course everyone's company. You've all been so kind.'

De Silva felt his heart go out to her. She had chosen her bed, but it couldn't be an easy one to lie in. He thought back to what Arthur had told Jane about the couple's argument. It was still possible that Alec and Belinda had been talking about something completely different. If, however, Arthur had stumbled on the truth, the Wragges leaving soon didn't give him much time to investigate.

'I expect you'll be busy getting ready, Belinda,' said Jane kindly.

Belinda sighed and looked sideways at Alec who, seemingly still preoccupied with his own thoughts, took no notice. 'Yes, there are travel arrangements to be made and as we've been here for quite a long time, Alec has written so many notes. They'll need a suitcase to themselves, and where we can put them when we get home, I really don't know.'

Alec roused himself to shoot her an angry look and she fell silent. De Silva wondered if notes would be all that was in their luggage. Yes, it would be a great mistake to let the Wragges go without further investigation.

* * *

'Well, what did you make of all that?' asked Jane when they were back in their quarters.

'I'm not sure yet. I know some post was delivered today and I'm afraid I've probably missed the chance to find out if there was a letter for the Wragges, but whether there was or not, I'm convinced that we shouldn't discount them, even if we do think Soma is the more likely thief, perhaps with Madeleine helping him.'

'I think you're right. It's lucky that Madeleine came back straight after dinner. At least we know where she is for the moment.'

De Silva sighed. 'I suppose that's to the good.'

'It's still early. Shall we wait for a while before we get ourselves organised to follow Madeleine if we have to?'

'Very well.'

An hour later, Jane finished her crossword, and de Silva closed his book. As quietly as they could, they put two of the chairs in the room together so that the seats faced each other and were only a little way apart. De Silva looked doubtfully at the new arrangement. He didn't want to say anything to Jane, but he foresaw a restless night. Still, at least that might make it easier to stay alert.

Jane went to the bedroom and came back with a pillow, one of the grey blankets from their bed, and a cream blanket that she had found in a box underneath it. 'It's a pity we didn't notice this one before,' she said. 'It's beautifully soft. I think it must be made from the hair of those goats rather than sheep's wool.'

She folded the grey blanket from their bed and placed it on one of the chair seats. 'I suggest you spread it out to lie on when you're ready to sleep.' She plumped the pillow and put it down at one end then draped the soft blanket over one of the arms before going to look out of the window. To her left, there was a square of light on the verandah.

'Madeleine can't have blown out her candles yet. I think she often stays up quite late. I'll leave the shutters ajar.'

'You go to bed if you like.'

'No, I'll wait with you until she turns in. I have another crossword I can do to pass the time.'

Another hour passed before the square of light on the verandah disappeared. 'I'm going to the bedroom,' whispered Jane. 'I've had an idea.'

She returned with a small pot. 'Talcum powder. I'll sprinkle a little outside our door in case Madeleine gets up and you don't hear her. If there are footprints in the morning, at least we'll know she went out.'

'But what if she notices it and asks questions?'

'Oh, I'll say I spilled some on one of my skirts and shook it off outside, knowing Anzan or Chatura would sweep the verandah in the morning.'

'Ha! Good thinking,' said Shanti.

She took off the lid of the pot and de Silva smelled lavender. Once she had sprinkled a little of the powder on the verandah floor, she came back inside.

'There, that's done.' She kissed de Silva on the cheek. 'Sleep well, dear. Unless Madeleine wakes you up, of course. You will wake me if she does, won't you?'

'I promise.'

Jane retired to the bedroom and de Silva heard her moving about getting ready for bed. He had resolved to remove only his shoes and sleep in his clothes so that he was ready to move quickly if he needed to. He sat down on one of the chairs and pulled the other one towards him so that the seat was under his knees. It was lucky that the chairs had quite deep seats. He wouldn't have to curl up too uncomfortably.

The chairs sagged a little as he tried to arrange the grey blanket underneath himself in the way Jane had suggested and get into a comfortable position. When he decided he had done the best job of it that he could, he squashed the pillow under his head and pulled the soft blanket over him. A breath of rapidly cooling night air drifted in through the shutters. It would probably be at least an hour before the moon came up, yet as his eyes became accustomed to the darkness, he was able to make out the shapes of the things in the room. The little fireplace that must be a welcome feature for winter guests; the candles in their plain wooden candle-sticks on the mantelshelf; the low table where the book he had been reading and Jane's crossword book and sewing basket lay. He thought of Sunnybank with its comfortable, attractive furniture, pretty ornaments, well-polished silver and glass, and fragrant arrangements of fresh flowers. With luck, tonight would see some progress in getting to the bottom of this crime and he and Jane would soon be back in Nuala with Billy and Bella.

A soft scuffling sound outside banished the thought. He doubted Madeleine was sufficiently light-footed to make the noise. He pushed the cream blanket aside and sat up, swinging his bare feet soundlessly to the ground. Stealthily, he went to peer between the shutters. Two tiny shadows were moving about on the floor of the verandah. He guessed they were mice or maybe shrews. Back on his makeshift bed, as the scuffling continued, he fell into a doze.

Five hours later, he awoke with a jolt to see dawn light filtering through the shutters. Crossly, he sat up and rubbed his eyes; he had been so sure he wouldn't sleep that soundly. Then he remembered the talcum powder. Going to the door, he opened it cautiously. The fine white powder was criss-crossed with many footprints but to his relief, they were all far too tiny to belong to Madeleine.

CHAPTER 9

'Never mind, there was no harm done,' said Jane when she woke a little later on and came into the living room. 'I'll take the watch tonight, if you like.' She laughed. 'I'm not sure why you're looking so dubious. I may have a better chance than you of staying awake. At least thanks to the talcum powder we know Madeleine didn't go out.'

'Yes, we have that to be thankful for, but we'd better not use the same trick again tonight.'

'I agree. Now, let's put the blankets and the pillow back in the bedroom and move the chairs to their usual positions, or Anzan and Chatura will wonder what we've been doing.'

It only took a few moments to rearrange the room then de Silva sank down in one of the chairs. 'Oof! I may have slept deeply but these chairs have made me ache in muscles I never knew I had. Are you sure about being in here tonight?'

'Perfectly sure.'

De Silva glanced towards the door. 'I hope Anzan or Chatura won't be long with the hot water. Maybe I'll feel better once I've had a wash.'

Not long afterwards, Chatura arrived with a bowl of hot water and clean towels. De Silva washed and changed into fresh clothes then waited whilst Jane got ready.

'I've been thinking about Alec and Belinda Wragge,' he said when she emerged from the bedroom in a pale green, full-skirted dress with its collar and short sleeves piped at the edges in red.

'So have I, and a departure from their original plan would be suspicious even if Arthur hadn't mentioned overhearing them say something about a manuscript.' She paused. 'I wish I could remember Arthur's precise words now, although he may not have heard exactly what they said anyway. What do you propose to do?'

'Questioning them won't be enough. We need a search of their rooms, but in a place like this, it will be impossible to do that in secret, even if it were proper. I'm conscious that strictly speaking, my authority here is uncertain. Before I do anything, I ought to speak to Soma and Gunananda, as a matter of courtesy if nothing else.'

'Do you think they'll object?'

'I hope not. If they do, I'll have to do my best to get around that.' He reached for his shoes and put them on. 'Shall we go to breakfast? After that I'll try to make a suitable arrangement.'

* * *

Chatura served them at breakfast. Madeleine was absent as usual and there was no sign of the Wragges. Arthur was also elsewhere.

'Perhaps he's gone out on one of his early morning plant-hunting expeditions,' said Jane when Chatura had brought tea and gone out again to fetch their food. 'He told me he likes to be back before the day gets too hot.'

'It's just as well really. It means I can't give in to the temptation to ask him if he's heard any more from the Wragges.'

'Yes, he would be bound to wonder why we're interested in them, and if they are innocent, it would be very unfair to have blackened their name.'

Chatura returned with two plates and placed them in front of de Silva and Jane. De Silva looked at the fried eggs glistening appetisingly on them. 'My goodness, what have we here?'

'Jungle fowl eggs, sahib,' said Chatura with a grin. 'Bhante Soma gave some of us the job of collecting them in the forest.'

'Well, they look delicious. We'd better eat them whilst they're hot.' At least something was going well today, he thought as he tucked in.

* * *

Breakfast over, de Silva sent Chatura to ask if Soma and Gunananda would see him. A message soon came back asking him to come in one hour's time. 'Wish me luck,' he said to Jane as he set off.

Gunananda was on his own. 'Bhante Soma should have been here by now,' he said. 'He must have been delayed, but we can begin our talk provided you do not mind repeating a few things when he comes.' He gave a self-deprecating smile. 'My memory sometimes fails me.'

'It comes to us all,' said de Silva, returning the smile.

'Please, sit.' Gunananda indicated a low stool. De Silva reflected that he didn't look as overwhelmed by distress as Soma had indicated, although to be fair, it was possible he would reveal more to Soma than he would to a virtual stranger. He cast around for where to begin.

'I want to speak to you about your guests Alec Wragge and his wife Belinda.'

'The young couple,' said Gunananda with a nod. 'I expect Soma will know more about them than I do.' He cupped a hand to his ear. 'Ah, I hear footsteps. Perhaps this is him now.'

Bhante Gunananda's memory might be failing but his hearing wasn't, thought de Silva. The door opened and Soma strode into the room. De Silva began to get to his feet, but the monk motioned him to sit again. 'Good morning, I'm sorry to have kept you waiting.'

'There's no need to apologise.'

'The inspector has come to see us about Alec Wragge and his wife,' said Gunananda.

'Oh? Do you think they have anything to do with this? I suppose he has an interest in old manuscripts, but he came to study our Buddhist texts, not medieval manuscripts. How do you suggest he would know that Bartholomew Parry's manuscript was here?'

'I can't answer that, but I'm concerned that he and his wife have decided to leave sooner than they planned. They may have something to do with the theft. I think a search of their quarters before they go would be advisable, but I didn't want to take steps to carry one out without consulting you first.'

'Is the change in their departure your only grounds for suspecting them?'

Once more de Silva wished he knew what was going on behind those penetrating eyes.

Soma cleared his throat and got to his feet. He turned to Gunananda. 'Are you happy for this search to take place?'

'What do you think?' asked Gunananda in a tentative voice.

Soma paused for a moment before he spoke, and de Silva wondered if he was going to argue but then he gave a perfunctory nod. 'I doubt it will come to anything, but search if you want. I insist, however, that I tell the Wragges in my own way why the search is being done. I don't want them knowing too much about the manuscript. That way, we can at least pay some respect to Bartholomew Parry's memory.'

* * *

Half an hour passed, and de Silva began to feel restless. Bhante Gunananda hadn't spoken for some time. He sat very still with such a blank expression on his face that de Silva assumed he had taken refuge in meditation from the unpleasant situation. He wondered whether he should leave and wait in the courtyard. Perhaps Soma was having difficulty finding the Wragges. But then he heard footsteps. The door opened and Soma came in. He glanced at Gunananda then stepped outside again, beckoning de Silva to follow him.

'I'm sorry you had to wait so long,' he said when they were far enough away not to disturb Gunananda. 'Alec Wragge has refused to be present, but Belinda is waiting for you. I took the liberty of finding your wife and asking her to help. I think it would be seemlier if she searches Belinda's personal possessions, don't you?'

'I agree.'

There was no sound from Arthur Warrender's rooms as they passed by. In the Wragges' sitting room, Belinda was perched on the edge of one of the chairs, her hands tightly clenched in her lap; she looked drained. 'If this manuscript you're looking for is here,' she said, 'it will be a mistake. Alec would never steal anything, I promise you. He might have brought something back to study, but he would always have returned it.' Her voice faltered.

Jane put a hand on her shoulder. 'No one is accusing either of you. Shanti just needs to be thorough. The manuscript is a valuable one.'

'Would you like to begin your search?' asked Soma. He gave Belinda a reassuring smile. 'It shouldn't take long.'

De Silva wondered if his confidence stemmed from the fact that he knew perfectly well that they would find nothing.

'May I go into your bedroom, Belinda?' asked Jane. Belinda nodded dumbly. She remained in her chair and Soma went to stand by the window, seemingly engrossed in the view of the courtyard. He was right, thought de Silva, searching this room wouldn't take long. There were so few pieces of furniture. He did however roll back the rug in the middle of the floor so that he could look carefully at all the wooden boards. None of them looked as if they had been disturbed. There was no sign of any papers or other work that he would have expected Alec Wragge to have with him. Perhaps it was already packed. The only books in sight were a couple of sixpenny Penguin paperbacks. He read the cover of the one on top: an English translation of Homer's *Odyssey*.

'That's Alec's,' said Belinda. 'He says I only read rubbish,' she added sadly.

De Silva left her with Soma and moved on to the washroom, but he found nothing there. He stood at the door to the bedroom to watch Jane. 'How are you getting on?' he asked quietly.

'Pretty well, there isn't much more to do.' She pointed to a small pile of luggage. 'Those two suitcases and the holdall have clothes and shoes in them.'

'What about papers?'

'They're probably in there.' She indicated a small trunk. 'Why don't you make a start on it?'

De Silva went to the trunk, knelt down, and snapped open the brass locks. He lifted the lid to find that the trunk wasn't as full as he had expected. By the look of it, Alec hadn't really amassed all that much research to take away with him. He lifted the contents out and divided them in two piles. Jane came to kneel beside him, and they started to look through them. It was soon obvious that there was nothing incriminating. Carefully, they replaced the papers then got to their feet.

'Shall we go and talk to Belinda now?' asked Jane.

'Yes. We'd better ask what she and Alec were talking about when Arthur Warrender overheard them.'

Belinda looked up sharply when they came back into the sitting room. She seemed a little more confident and de Silva glimpsed a flash of defiance in her eyes. 'There's nothing wrong, is there? I knew there wouldn't be. I'd like to get on with our packing now.'

'All in good time,' said de Silva in the most soothing voice he could manage. 'I need to ask you something first.'

'Oh?'

'A few nights ago, Arthur Warrender overheard you arguing with your husband and trying to dissuade him from doing "the wrong thing". Can you explain what that was about?'

Belinda shivered. 'Arthur told you we were arguing, did he? Horrible man. He pretends to be nice and friendly but he's always nosing around. I won't be sorry to leave him behind.'

A look of great bitterness swept across her face. Her eyes were moist. 'I don't remember those exact words, but if you must know, we were arguing about Alec's work, and now what I feared would happen has done. The university have written to tell him they aren't renewing his research grant. Alec was so angry that he tore the letter up on the spot. He was all for having an argument with the principal when we got home, but I've manged to persuade him that it would only make things worse. If he can't get a fellowship somewhere else, he'll have to give up and try to get a place as a schoolmaster, which he'll hate. All the work that he's done since he went back to the university after the war will have been for nothing.'

She took out a handkerchief and dabbed her eyes. 'He had what some people call "a good war" but they don't understand. Alec didn't pass the medical board. He has flat feet, so they said he wouldn't be able to march. He ended up with a desk job, and much as I tried to cheer him up, he kept saying he was a failure. I hoped he'd be happier after we were married but it hasn't made any difference.' She blew her nose resolutely then scrunched the handkerchief into a ball, squeezing it until her knuckles turned white. 'And now this blow about his work.'

'I'm very sorry to hear it, ma'am.'

'We'll leave you in peace now,' said Jane.

Belinda stood up, her back ramrod straight and her expression unsmiling. 'Thank you.'

* * *

'Oh dear,' said Jane as, back in their own apartment, she closed the door, 'what a terrible mess. Let's hope Alec enjoys life as a schoolmaster better than he thinks he will. I know I found teaching very rewarding.' She kicked off her shoes and went to sit down on one of the chairs. 'Well, what do we do now? I think we can take it that the Wragges aren't involved in the theft, don't you?'

'Yes. I'll speak with Soma and Gunananda and let them know we didn't find anything. What interests me now is what Arthur Warrender was up to when he told you about their argument. Did his remark spring from innocent concern, or did he have an ulterior motive?'

'You mean was he hoping to throw suspicion on the Wragges? From what Belinda told us, he might have been putting words into her mouth too and if that's right, it suggests that he knows the manuscript's missing and we're looking for it.'

De Silva nodded. 'And from there it's a reasonable conclusion that he's the person we're after. I think it's time we looked into Mr Warrender.'

'Oh, Shanti, that's shocking! He's a clergyman.'

'I fear that's not necessarily a guarantee of honesty, my love. I recall that Inspector Singh once had to deal with a Hatton vicar who embezzled the parish funds.'

Jane's brow furrowed. 'Oh dear me, now that you mention it, I remember. It was a dreadful business.' She thought for a moment. 'Of course we only have his word for it that he is a clergyman. Do you remember when I asked him at supper one evening where his parish in England had been? I thought I might have known it.'

'Vaguely.'

'He knocked a glass of water over and there was a bit of a kerfuffle mopping it up. It may have been an accident, but it might have been deliberate. Afterwards, he asked me where I'd worked and then said his parish had been a long way off from there.'

'You think he wanted you to give him the name of the parish you lived in first? That's a good point.'

'Perhaps Reverend Peters could help us here. He's bound to have a copy of *Crockfords Clerical Directory*. If Arthur Warrender really is a vicar, his name should be in there. It's not a very common one, and that ought to help.'

'It's probably time I made that visit to Nuala anyway. I don't see much prospect of our leaving here by the time we planned. I can visit Archie and go to Sunnybank to reassure the servants we haven't fallen down the mountainside. It wouldn't do any harm to check up on Prasanna and Nadar either. I expect they're managing perfectly well without me, but I don't want them getting too comfortable with that.'

'I'll stay here as we agreed and try to keep an eye on Arthur, and Soma and Madeleine too.'

De Silva paused. He had briefly forgotten Soma and Madeleine. If they were guilty and decided to make a move, he didn't like the idea of Jane having to deal with them on her own. 'You will be careful, won't you?'

'You don't need to worry about me.'

'But I do.'

She kissed his cheek. 'Thank you, dear, but please don't. I won't do anything rash like taking on Madeleine and Soma singlehanded.'

'How did you know that was what was on my mind?'

Jane laughed. 'After all these years, it's not very difficult to work out what you're thinking.' She sighed. 'If any of them are the people we want, I hope they make a move soon. We seem to have been a long time away from everything at home, and of course Billy and Bella.'

'Yes, I miss those little rascals too. I promise to give them your love.'

CHAPTER 10

Jane still insisted on being the one to sleep in the living room that night. De Silva had to admit he was quite relieved to be spared another restless one. In bed, he stretched out and wriggled his toes. The monastery's mattress was thin, but it was undoubtedly more comfortable than the chairs in the living room. He turned his mind to his conversation earlier that evening with Soma. When de Silva had told him that he no longer suspected the Wragges, he had promised to pass the information on to Gunananda but expressed neither surprise nor disappointment. De Silva wondered whether that was because Soma had never expected anything to be found, as he already knew exactly what had happened to the manuscript. *If he and Madeleine make a move*, thought de Silva, *I might have the answer to that question by morning*. Rolling over onto his side, he curled up and was soon fast asleep.

He woke to find Jane standing over him, shaking him by the shoulder. 'Shanti,' she whispered. 'Wake up, I've heard something next door.'

Groggily, he rubbed his eyes. After his previous bad night and the difficult day with the Wragges, he had been dead to the world. He concentrated on keeping his eyes open and listening to the sounds in the adjoining room. Unmistakeably, someone was moving about in there. It must be Madeleine. Was she getting ready to go out to meet Soma? With a flicker of anticipation, he sat up and swung his legs over the side of the bed. Jane was rapidly dressing, and he followed suit.

When they were ready, they both went quietly to the living room and listened at the door to the verandah. Through the shutters, de Silva saw a faint light. He was fairly sure that the moon wouldn't be up so Madeleine must have a light of some kind, perhaps a torch.

Jane nudged him and put a finger to her lips as Madeleine's door softly opened and closed. Quiet footsteps passed theirs. They waited until the sound had faded before slipping out themselves in time to see her crossing the courtyard, keeping to the edge, a moving pinprick of light in the darkness. She disappeared in the direction of the path up the mountain; fortunately, she hadn't looked back.

De Silva turned on their own torch but shielded the beam with his hand. 'Go carefully,' he said. 'We don't want any stumbles on that rocky path.'

Jane sniffed. 'I'm as sure-footed as you.' He squeezed her hand. 'It wasn't a criticism,' he murmured under his breath. At the rise onto the mountain path, they waited until they had located the pinprick of light once more. Madeleine was walking fast. She had already climbed to the first place in the path where a narrow track led off to strike out across the side of the mountain. She did not, however, take that one, but went on to the next branch in the path before leaving it and taking a route Shanti had not tried previously.

'It may be hard following her,' de Silva whispered to Jane. 'If she turns to look back, she's almost certain to spot us.'

'We'll just have to be ready to stop. It's much harder to see a stationary object in the dark,' Jane whispered back. 'Anyway, I'm not sure she will. She seems very intent on getting to wherever she's going.'

They waited until Madeleine was a good distance ahead

before setting off again. From all sides of the track there came the throb of night insects. The warm air was scented with herbs and other aromatic plants. This could have been an enjoyable walk, thought de Silva, if he hadn't been so apprehensive about what they might find at the end of it and if the stones on the track hadn't been attacking his feet through the soles of his shoes. He clenched his jaw to stop himself making any noise when he encountered a particularly sharp one.

At last the pinprick of light came to a halt by what looked like a tall outcrop of rock and then vanished. De Silva's heart missed a beat. Jane tapped him on the shoulder but when he turned, he could barely make out her features in the darkness. 'I think she's arrived at her destination,' she whispered. 'If she's meeting Soma, let's hope he got there first.'

The last section of track that they had to negotiate seemed endless and was very overgrown. De Silva trod even more carefully than before, mindful of hidden holes or low bushes that might trip him up, but at last they reached the place where the light had disappeared.

On the far side of the outcrop, a few yards ahead of them, taller bushes grew around what seemed to be an opening in the rock. There must be a cave. The murmur of voices was coming from inside it. One of them belonged to Madeleine and the other was undoubtedly Soma's, but they were speaking too quietly for de Silva to make out what they were saying. He switched off his torch. Suddenly, he wished he hadn't let Jane come on this expedition with him. Soma was meant to be a man of peace, but what if they were about to expose him as a criminal? How would he react? Would there be a fight? All he had was a torch and his fists, and Soma was a much younger man. If the monk prevailed, how was he going to defend Jane?

At the point where they stood, the path was angled

more steeply towards the downward slope than it had been before. Unconsciously he shifted his weight, and a loose stone rolled from under his foot, setting off a little avalanche amongst its neighbours. Abruptly, the murmur of voices stopped. De Silva held his breath until it started again, then after what was probably no more than a minute but felt like an hour, Jane tugged at his sleeve and brought her lips close to his ear. 'We have to go in.'

Madeleine's voice drifted out of the cave. 'I'm sure there's something out there, Soma. Go and see what it is.'

Silence again, then de Silva heard a rustling sound. He tensed, ready to grapple with Soma if he had to. The monk's tall figure emerged from the darkness and the beam of the torch he carried explored his surroundings. It paused at the place where de Silva and Jane stood; de Silva shaded his eyes as it dazzled him.

'What is it?' hissed Madeleine from inside the cave.

'What are you doing here?' snapped Soma. His expression threatening, he took a step forward. As Madeleine followed him out of the cave, de Silva prepared himself for a fight, but she put a restraining hand on Soma's arm.

'Calm down, Soma. Give Shanti and Jane a chance to explain. Let's go back inside.'

Grudgingly, Soma acquiesced and as they all moved into the surprisingly roomy cave, embarrassment overcame de Silva. If all there was to this was that Soma and Madeleine were in love, this was going to be awkward, but he had to be honest. Torchlight gave the cave an eerie quality. 'Well, come on then,' Soma said coldly.

'On the morning that you told me about the theft, I went up early to the lake to see the sunrise. As I came down, I saw a couple walking in front of me. I thought I recognised both of you and wondered what you were doing there at such an early hour.'

Madeleine looked at Soma crossly. 'I told you we

shouldn't have left it so late to return to the monastery that morning. Didn't I say we'd risk being seen?'

Soma shrugged. 'And as usual you were right, but it hardly matters now, does it?' He faced de Silva again. 'Why would our private meetings interest you enough to have you running around the mountainside in the dark?' He paused then his expression took on a hint of dry amusement. 'Ah, I see, you put two and two together and made five. You think our meetings have something to do with the theft of the manuscript, am I right? Madeleine knows all about it, so I can speak freely and assure you that neither of us are the thief.'

Madeleine was smiling too, but de Silva wasn't yet ready to relax his guard.

'I think we'd better go down and talk about this in my quarters where we can be more comfortable,' she said. 'Anyway, it will soon be time for the monks to rise, and it would never do for the four of us to be seen together out here.'

* * *

In Madeleine's quarters, de Silva noticed that the living room furnishings were as spartan as his and Jane's, but a plethora of lusciously hued silk and cashmere scarves had been draped everywhere, lending the room an air of bohemian luxury. Both she and Soma were dressed in dark clothing. She sat down in one of the chairs, looking so composed that it was hard to believe that she had just been surprised in a clandestine meeting on a mountainside. Soma stood by the fireplace with one arm resting casually on the mantelshelf. He might have been a gentleman who was entertaining visitors. The situation had an air of unreality to it.

Madeleine indicated the other chairs. 'Do make yourselves comfortable. Soma, shall we have a drink? I think we could all do with one. The walk from that cave is very tedious. Make mine a whisky, please.'

Soma went to the small cupboard in one corner of the room and opened the door. On one of the shelves was a selection of glasses and bottles.

'Are you shocked?' asked Madeleine with a mischievous smile. 'I always bring something with me. For medicinal purposes, of course. What will you have?'

Feeling even more bemused, de Silva accepted a whisky and Jane a sherry. Soma poured their drinks and brought them over but didn't take one for himself.

'Will you explain, Soma, or shall I?' asked Madeleine.

'I'll do it.' Soma picked up the bundle of papers on the low table in the middle of the room and handed them to Jane before returning to the fireplace. He raised an eyebrow. 'You may as well know our secret. I hope that when you do, you'll agree to keep it to yourselves.'

Jane picked up the top sheet of paper and looked at it. 'A novel? I don't understand.'

'I'm not surprised,' said Madeleine with a chuckle. 'I imagine that you were thinking of all sorts of reasons why we might want to meet in secret, and that's perfectly understandable. Who would expect to find a Buddhist monk who writes adventure stories with a little help from a romantic novelist?'

'More than a little help,' said Soma with a smile. 'Let me explain. When I came to the monastery, I soon realised that it was in decline. As I became more senior, I decided that I would like to do something about that. My problem was, however, where to find the money to carry out my plans.'

'That's where I came in,' said Madeleine. 'Soma and I knew each other in his previous life. I hope he won't mind my saying that it was a rather hedonistic one.'

Soma laughed. 'If that means I spent far too much time enjoying myself, I have to agree.'

'He also dabbled in writing, something that created a bond between us. I suggested that he take it up again.'

'When Madeleine comes to the monastery each year, rather than working on her own books all the time as she tells everyone, she also edits my work and adds a dash of romance. We meet in secret from time to time to decide on the final version of the latest book. She then takes the manuscript back to Colombo and arranges for it to be published under the pen name of Charles Castlemaine.'

'Gracious!' said Jane. 'Then I've seen your books in libraries and bookshops. They're very popular.'

Soma smiled. 'You're too kind.'

Madeleine finished her whisky. 'You know they're popular, my dear. No need to be modest. And whilst they are, the monastery benefits.'

'Does Bhante Gunananda know about all of this?' asked de Silva.

'Gracious no,' said Madeleine. 'It's harmless of course, but it seemed better not to involve him.'

Soma gave de Silva and Jane a searching look. 'So, the question now is, what will you do with this information? I'd be grateful if you would keep it to yourselves, but of course you must make up your own minds.'

Jane and de Silva looked at each other. 'I think Shanti will agree that the last thing we would want to do is interfere with your good intentions,' said Jane. De Silva nodded.

Soma placed the palms of his hands together and gave them a low bow. 'Thank you, from the bottom of my heart.' He looked grave. 'So now that you've ruled out the Wragges, Madeleine, and me, who do you have left in your sights?'

De Silva decided not to mention that he and Jane had also considered Anzan. He'd rather deal with Anzan's problems later.

'Arthur Warrender.'

'The clergyman?' Soma looked surprised.

'I'm afraid that's not a guarantee of honesty.'

'I suppose not.'

'I'd like to find out more about him, and for that I need to go back to Nuala for a day or two. Jane will stay here, and if anyone asks she can explain that I've been called away on police business.'

'We promise to take great care of her,' said Madeleine with a smile.

* * *

'Well, that was the last thing I was expecting,' said Jane as they returned to their apartment. Beyond the verandah, the monastery buildings stood like silent witnesses to the final hour before the monks rose to commence their day. Jane pulled her light cardigan around her. 'It's chilly at this time of night. If we hadn't been in such a hurry to keep up with Madeleine, I would have found something warmer to put on.'

De Silva thought that he hadn't noticed the cold. He felt calmer now, but the night's events had kept him quite warm enough. Indeed, when he'd seen Soma coming out of that cave, his heart had started to pump the blood through his veins at such a rate that it could have been high noon on the hottest day of the year.

'I'll set off for Nuala once I've had a bit of sleep,' he said. 'I'll talk to Reverend Peters, and fill Archie in on what's been going on. Then last but not least, I'll go to Sunnybank and see how our little rascals are getting on.'

* * *

They slept for a few hours, and when they woke, decided not to go to the dining room for breakfast.

'I don't know about you, but if Arthur's there, I'd rather not have to answer any questions about our plans for the day,' said de Silva.

'I agree. Anzan and Chatura are bound to be somewhere about. If we don't turn up, I expect one of them will come to see if we need anything. I'll go out later and if I meet anyone who asks where you are, I'll tell them the story about your being called back to Nuala for a day or two on police business.'

De Silva made a face. 'If Arthur's our man, let's hope he swallows it.'

Jane gave him a little punch on the arm. 'I can be very convincing when I want to be.'

He grinned. 'I know.' He picked up his watch from the bedside table and glanced at the time. 'Maybe I'll get off now and stop on the way for some breakfast. That should give me time to see at least one of Archie or Reverend Peters today, so with luck I'll be back here by tomorrow evening at the latest.'

'Good idea.'

CHAPTER 11

De Silva took the winding road down the mountain carefully. In the early morning light the forest on either side looked gloomy, but he saw occasional flashes of purple and red where rhododendrons shouldered up between the trees. When he reached the valley, he speeded up, recalling that the road passed through a place called Oyagama. It had looked to be somewhere where one might be able to find breakfast.

Forest gave way to palms and banana trees, but eventually even those began to thin out to make way for a few roadside shacks. Outside many of them, small patches of ground had been cultivated to grow vegetables. Goats were tethered by some of the shacks, and children who seemed to be well fed, even though their clothes were ragged, were playing. They looked up as he passed and waved. Some of them ran after the Morris but soon tired of the game.

When he reached the centre of the village, de Silva found a little market in progress. The produce on offer was far more limited than it would have been in Nuala, but the fruit and vegetables looked fresh and there were a good number of sacks of lentils, rice, maize, and spices. Some of the stalls had canopies of sacking and there were even a few with tin roofs. He guessed that the village was fairly prosperous, unlike many of the jungle ones. He wondered what would happen to them all if the British left the island.

He felt sure now that they would, although their departure might still be several years away.

He parked the Morris and gave a few annas to two boys who were eying her admiringly, with a promise of more if no harm had come to her by the time he came back. It was a precaution he no longer resorted to in Nuala but there most people knew the Morris belonged to the chief of police and he felt she was safe enough.

The first food stall he came to offered only dahl and rice, so he moved on, hoping he would be able to find somewhere to satisfy his craving for a good vegetable curry. He found it three stalls away, where a steaming, blackened iron pot contained chunks of okra and jackfruit studded with plenty of fresh green chillies and fragrant with curry leaves, turmeric, and cumin. He paid for a large bowl with rice then took it over to a small area in the shade where a few cheap metal tables and chairs had been set up. As he savoured the first few mouthfuls, he thought guiltily of Jane. He hoped it was a day when the monastery's usual offering of dahl was augmented by some of their goats' cheese or an egg or two from the jungle fowl.

From where he sat, he saw the stream that gave the village its name. Children were playing there, paddling in the water, and splashing each other. The sound of their carefree chatter and laughter added to the hum of noise from the bazaar. He had almost finished his meal and was wondering whether to have a second helping when he noticed that some of the children by the stream were running towards the road that passed the bazaar. Other customers sitting at the tables around him or browsing their way along stalls looked in the same direction, shading their eyes against the sun. De Silva did the same and saw a Land Rover turning off the road and coming to a halt close to where he had left the Morris. Obviously, the arrival of two motor cars in one morning was a notable event in Oyagama.

The driver, a man wearing a beige suit and a Panama hat that shaded his face from view, climbed out. As de Silva had done, he picked out a couple of lads to watch the car and a few coins were handed over, but instead of coming into the bazaar he strode off in the direction of a low, tin-roofed house that had a wooden verandah across its whitewashed façade and looked a little more affluent than its neighbours. A sign over the door announced that it was a hotel. As he stepped inside, the driver took off his hat, revealing grey hair. He was gone too quickly for de Silva to see his face clearly, but something stirred in his memory.

'Shall I fetch more food for you, sahib?' De Silva looked up to see a young lad smiling hopefully at him. No doubt he would like a tip as the price of this service. He shook his head. 'No, but you can do something else for me.'

The flicker of disappointment that had dulled the lad's expression disappeared. 'Yes, sahib?'

'Can you find out who that man is who drove up in the Land Rover?'

'I can tell you that straight away, sahib,' the lad said proudly. 'He is Sahib Jim Aevens.'

'How do you know that?'

'My cousin works in the hotel. Sahib Aevens has been staying there.'

De Silva fished in his pocket, brought out a few annas and handed them over. 'Thank you.' He filed the name away in his memory. It was probably nothing; the clothes the man had been wearing were pretty much a uniform for British men in Ceylon, and plenty must have grey hair, but one never knew.

The lad beamed. '*Namaste*, sahib.'

* * *

It was almost one o'clock by the time de Silva reached Nuala. He decided that his visit to the police station could wait until morning and drove straight to Sunnybank. He let himself into the hall and called out a greeting. For a moment no one answered, then one of the servants appeared from the direction of the kitchen. She looked a little apprehensive but the moment she saw de Silva, a big smile lit her face.

'Welcome, sahib!'

'Hello, Delisha. How are you?'

Delisha's smile vanished. 'Oh, sahib, we have nothing prepared for you. If only we had known that you were coming home today. Leela is here but Jayasena has taken cook to town in the memsahib's car to do some shopping. The memsahib said that would be alright.'

'Never mind. It's unfortunate I wasn't able to give you any warning, but I had a good breakfast. Anyway, I probably won't be staying long. I have some business to see to, but I hope to go back to the monastery tomorrow. The memsahib is still up there.'

'Then cook will make something special for your dinner tonight, sahib.'

'I look forward to it. For now, an omelette will do.' He glanced around the hall. 'So, where's the rest of the welcoming committee?'

Delisha chuckled. 'I expect they are with Leela. She's in the scullery. The memsahib wanted all the silver cleaned whilst you were away.'

De Silva followed Delisha back to the kitchen and down the passage to the scullery. When he opened the door, the astringent smell of silver polish wafted towards him. Leela looked up, her cloth poised over the lid of the ornate silver teapot that she was polishing.

'Sahib!'

'Don't let me stop you working, Leela. I seem to have

caused enough consternation already. Are you well?'

'Very well, thank you, sahib.' The girl smiled. 'If you're looking for Billy and Bella, they ran out to the garden a few minutes ago.'

'Ah good, that's where I planned to go myself.' It would be lunchtime at the Residence so best not to telephone Archie yet. 'I'll go and find them,' he went on. 'Is Anif out there as well?'

'Yes, sahib. He said he would be working in the vegetable garden.'

De Silva went out by the back door and walked around the house and across the lawn towards the far end of the garden. As he reached the path that led to the vegetable plots, two familiar black shapes came running to meet him, tails held high and sleek black fur gleaming in the sunshine. He bent down to stroke them.

'Hello, you two, have you missed me? I'm afraid you'll have to wait a bit longer for Jane to come home.'

Bella remained beside him, nuzzling up against his hand and purring, whilst Billy, more independent as usual, sauntered off to a mat of leaves and vanished under it.

Anif came around the corner of the potting shed with the wheelbarrow. He waggled his head. 'Good afternoon, sahib.'

He put the barrow down and lifted out a fork and a trug. 'The last of these aubergines are ready to pick, sahib. When that is done, I'll clear the bed.'

De Silva felt amused. Anif didn't appear surprised by his sudden reappearance, even though it was rare for him to be away for long, but then very little seemed to surprise him. 'Good idea. Billy will have to find another place to use as a hidey hole.'

Anif took a curved knife from the pouch on his belt and began to cut away the shiny fruits. Some were of the common variety that was such a dark purple that it was almost black, but there were other varieties that de Silva had decided to try for a change, one a deep claret colour streaked with white, and the other creamy coloured. As Anif worked, they discussed what to plant next in the bed, and decided on tomatoes.

'I'll leave you to get on,' said de Silva eventually.

Anif nodded. 'Thank you, sahib.' He gave one of his rare smiles. 'It is good to have you back.'

Back at the house, cook prepared de Silva's omelette and he sat on the verandah to eat it. Just after two o'clock, he telephoned the Residence and was told that Archie was due back from Kandy but would be busy for the rest of the day when he arrived. He made an appointment to speak to him in the morning then dialled the number for the vicarage. The vicar's wife answered. It would be a great pleasure to see him. After he had discussed his business with her husband, de Silva must stay to tea.

CHAPTER 12

At the monastery, Jane changed her mind and decided to go to breakfast after all. Arthur Warrender would probably notice Shanti's absence anyway, so she might as well meet any questions head on.

When she went to the dining room, she was glad to find that the Wragges were also there. Alec Wragge was as morose as ever, but Belinda made a brave effort at conversation that made it easier than it would otherwise have been to move the subject on from de Silva's absence.

After breakfast was over, they all returned to their quarters. Jane decided to stay there until she heard Arthur go out, but if he did, she hoped he wouldn't go too far away. It would be difficult to follow him if he went on one of his forest expeditions. Fortunately he seemed disinclined to do so, and at lunchtime they met once more in the dining room, but this time there was no sign of the Wragges.

'I don't expect anyone will miss Alec's company,' remarked Arthur, as he and Jane ate the usual repast of dahl. 'Although Belinda is a very pleasant young woman.' He lifted the spoonful he was about to eat. 'I must admit, I envy them the prospect of a change of diet, but it's a sad business.' He lowered his voice. 'I understand from Madeleine that Belinda confided something of their troubles to her. In my opinion the life of a schoolmaster isn't so bad, I've known many excellent ones who appear to enjoy it, but clearly Wragge hoped to make his mark on the academic world.'

The door opened and Anzan came in with a jug of fresh water. Jane thanked him as he put down the jug, wishing she and Shanti had been able to make progress with helping him. She must talk to Shanti about that when he returned, and agree when to approach Gunananda and Soma.

'Have you decided on a date to leave yourself?' she asked Arthur when Anzan had gone.

'Nothing definite yet, but I've reached a convenient place to pause in my work, so I really ought to make up my mind.'

The door opened again, and this time Anzan brought in a small earthenware dish. 'There is some cheese today,' he said.

Arthur rubbed his hands. 'Excellent, excellent,' he said a little too effusively. When the two of them were alone again, he cut a piece of the goat cheese for Jane and one for himself. 'Rather pungent as usual, I'm afraid, but a pleasant change all the same. I expect your husband is glad to be having one too.'

'Yes, we're blessed with a very good cook.'

'I believe you said at breakfast that Shanti won't be gone for long.'

'That's right. He thought it likely he'd be back tomorrow. As I said this morning, it's a relatively straightforward matter that he has to deal with. Once he's had a word with his sergeant, he should be able to leave everything to him and return here.'

'Good, his company is always a pleasure.'

'It's very kind of you to say so.'

'Not at all.'

They finished their meal and Arthur stood up, giving Jane a little bow. 'Well. I wish you a pleasant afternoon.'

'Will you be going out on one of your expeditions?'

'I think not. I'll rest in my room instead. The weather's too hot today to make exertion of any kind a pleasure.'

Jane stood up too. It would be as well to make sure that

Arthur was really going to rest in his room. Hopefully, he would keep to his word and stay there. 'I quite agree,' she said. 'I've already decided to spend the afternoon in the garden, but first I need to fetch a few things from our quarters.'

* * *

Once Arthur had walked away down the corridor that led to his apartment, Jane fetched her crossword book and the piece of embroidery she was working on and settled down in her favourite shady corner of the garden close to a fran-gipani tree. Its white, waxy, funnel-shaped flowers gave off an intensely sweet smell. She had seen the monks cut small branches from the tree to place on either side of the shrine as offerings to the Buddha.

'Always so industrious, Jane my dear.'

She looked up from her embroidery to see Madeleine outside the gate with her hand on the latch. Today she was resplendent in a long, loose purple dress with a turban to match that was secured by a gold brooch set with a large amethyst. On her feet she wore a pair of burgundy Turkish slippers that glittered with gold embroidery. 'May I join you?'

'Of course.' Jane put her embroidery aside and Madeleine came into the garden and sat down.

'This heat! I'm sure it's hotter today than usual. But at least out here there's a chance of a breath of air. My rooms are insufferable.' She fanned herself with a well-manicured hand. 'Please don't tell Soma that I can't bear to read another word of his manuscript this afternoon. It's no criticism of his work. I truly believe this is one of his best books so far.'

'I shall have to read it. But what a shame that the world will never know his real name.'

Madeleine shrugged. 'This is the life he chose.'

'I must admit, I'm intrigued as to why he did.'

Madeleine gave her a thoughtful look. 'I'm sure you are,' she said quietly. 'Can I rely on your discretion?'

'Of course.'

'I've known Soma since he was a boy. He was born in Colombo, the youngest son of a wealthy family. His father had business interests in common with mine and that was how we knew the family. Soma was a clever boy, but he didn't apply himself to his studies. It used to infuriate his father who hoped for great things from his sons. Soma's elder brother didn't disappoint him. Radesh was diligence itself and when he was old enough, worked hard in the family business. In contrast, Soma was bent on enjoying himself.'

Jane had difficulty picturing the version of Soma that Madeleine was describing. 'How did his father react?'

'He frequently threatened to cut him off without a penny if he didn't pull himself together, but Soma was always the favourite with the boys' mother and somehow she never failed to talk her husband round.'

'I imagine something very significant must have occurred to cause Soma to make such a radical change in his life.'

'It did, and sadly the circumstances were tragic.' Madeleine raised an eyebrow. 'I don't suppose it has escaped your notice that Soma is a very attractive man. In those days, youth was on his side too. He had black hair that he wore on the long side – another thing that infuriated his father who called it a foppish affectation. He dressed well, excelled at most sports, and drove a fast car. If there was a party going on, he was usually there.'

Two of the novice monks passed by the garden. Madeleine stopped talking and smiled at them, putting her hands together in the traditional greeting which they returned. Jane followed suit, then the monks went on in the direction of the main hall. 'I expect it's their turn to polish everything,' said Madeleine. She chuckled. 'The Soma of yesterday wouldn't have noticed if a place was inches thick in dust, but the Soma of today demands high standards.' She paused. 'Where was I?'

'You were saying that something tragic happened.'

'Yes, Soma had many girlfriends, but then he met my niece, Lucy. He was twenty-three and she was a year younger.' There was a catch in Madeleine's voice, then she fell silent for a moment, seeming to forget she wasn't alone. She had obviously been very fond of this girl, thought Jane.

With a visible effort, Madeleine rallied. 'My niece was a delightful girl,' she went on. 'Very pretty and vivacious with long fair hair and a petite figure. She and Soma fell deeply in love, something that pleased both of his parents, who looked on her as a steadying influence. My sister and her husband were not so happy. A marriage between a Sinhalese boy and a British girl was fraught with complications.' She glanced at Jane. 'Something that I'm sure you're all too well acquainted with.'

'Yes, but Shanti and I had the advantage of being considerably older and none of our parents were alive, which made everything easier.'

'Yes, I can see that, but I assume that you must have met with difficulties in some respects.'

'There have been times, but people are used to us now in our little society in Nuala. And if outsiders raise their eyebrows, one has to accept that one cannot please everyone.'

'That's very true. I've certainly never let myself be troubled by people who disapprove of me.'

Jane doubted that many people dared to criticise Madeleine to her face, or at all.

'I know that the other thing that worried my sister and her husband was Soma's reputation,' Madeleine continued. 'They feared the match might not last, but eventually Soma's charm and Lucy's determination won them round.

I'm convinced the marriage would have been a long and happy one had fate not intervened.'

'What happened?'

'They were on the way up to Kandy from Colombo when they were involved in a car crash. It wasn't Soma's fault. The other car was speeding, and its driver lost control. Soma was badly injured and had to spend weeks in hospital, but nothing could be done to save Lucy.'

'Oh, how dreadful.'

'It was. We were all devastated. As for Soma, when he left hospital, his parents were afraid he might do himself harm. We all were. No matter what any of us said, he was convinced he was to blame.'

Madeleine cast a glance at the clump of ginger lilies nearby and her expression clouded. 'I'm not fond of lilies. Their scent is too cloying, and they remind me of funerals.'

Jane took in the ensuing silence then gathered up her book and sewing. 'I've been sitting here all afternoon. I might take a short walk now that it's a little cooler. Would you like to join me?'

'You're not only industrious but practical,' said Madeleine, with a half-smile. 'One mustn't allow oneself to repine, must one? Nothing can bring Lucy back. I expect Soma still thinks of her, but I believe that here he's achieved a modicum of peace. We were all surprised when he announced his intention to become a monk, but perhaps nothing should ever surprise one.'

'No, I suppose it shouldn't. Being married to Shanti and hearing about his work has taught me that. People do the most unexpected things and often turn out to be not at all what they originally seemed to be.'

Madeleine's lips twitched. 'Does that little piece of wisdom only spring from hearing about his work? I find it hard to believe that you never get involved in what goes on.'

Jane laughed. 'Well, perhaps I do. Just a little bit.'

CHAPTER 13

The servant who answered the vicarage door to de Silva left him in the hall and went to tell Mrs Peters that he had arrived. She came to greet him a few minutes later, full of apologies.

'I'm afraid my husband is over at the church. When you telephoned, I'd forgotten that he has a meeting with one of the churchwardens this afternoon, but he shouldn't be long. Would you like to come and sit in the garden whilst you wait?'

'I'd be delighted to, and there's no need to apologise. I have plenty of time.'

'Good, then follow me.' She turned to the servant. 'I'm sure Inspector de Silva is thirsty after his drive here. Please bring some of that fresh lemonade to the garden.'

'Yes, memsahib.'

In the garden, Mrs Peters led the way to the stone-flagged terrace where they sat down in the shade of a large flowery parasol. Waterlilies covered the surface of the small pond nearby where dragonflies darted across the surface like tiny bolts of lightning. On the trellis behind it, a vigorous creeper that de Silva hadn't noticed on his previous visits bloomed with a profusion of lavender trumpet-shaped flowers.

'Morning Glory,' said Mrs Peters. 'I'm afraid it will probably pull that trellis down one day, but it really lives up to its name when it flowers.'

'Our name for it is Railway Creeper.'

'That also seems very appropriate,' said Mrs Peters with a smile. 'It does seem to make its way very determinedly through whatever is in its path, just like the trains in Ceylon.'

De Silva laughed. 'But perhaps a little faster.'

As they waited for their lemonade, de Silva admired the garden. It contained many native trees as did the one at Sunnybank, as well as hibiscus, lilies, and cannas, but the geraniums that de Silva knew Mrs Peters was very fond of added an English touch, filling several flowerbeds with a ruched mass of pink, scarlet and white.

'When we came here, I was very glad to find that geraniums grow so well in this country,' she remarked when he complimented her on them. She sighed. 'Time flies, doesn't it? That was many years ago and it seems like yesterday.' She surveyed the garden. 'I suppose one day we shall have to leave all this. I'll miss it so much.'

'I hope that day will be a long way off, ma'am.'

'Thank you, but I know it will come. I hope we'll be able to stay in Ceylon. It seems far more like home than England does now, but since the war, so much has changed.'

Her expression was wistful. He was sure she was thinking of the troubles in India. The British government that had been elected after the war was prepared to grant the country the independence that the Nationalists had fought for so long to obtain. However, violence between the Hindu, Sikh, and Muslim communities whose leaders could not agree on the shape of an independent state was making the prospect of a united India ever more distant. He supposed an answer would be found eventually, and when India achieved independence Ceylon would follow, but he prayed that his homeland's rebirth would be a peaceful one.

A different servant to the one who had greeted de Silva appeared, carrying a silver tray on which were two tall glasses and a jug of lemonade garnished with mint. She placed it on the table and de Silva smelled a refreshing citrusy tang.

'Shall I bring anything else, memsahib?' asked the servant when she had poured out the lemonade.

Mrs Peters turned to de Silva. 'Are you hungry, Inspector?'

'Thank you, ma'am, but it's not long since I had lunch at home.'

'Ah, then perhaps it's best to wait for teatime. I hope you'll be hungry by then. Cook and I have been baking this morning.'

'Then I have a great treat in store.'

Mrs Peters nodded to the servant. 'Thank you, Dayani. That will be all for the moment. Now,' she went on when the servant had withdrawn, 'I'd like to hear about your visit to this monastery. Soma, the monk who came to visit us a while ago, was a most interesting man, and I know Jane was very much looking forward to seeing the place for herself. I've even been wondering if I might persuade my husband to undertake a visit.' She looked thoughtful. 'Perhaps when he retires, although of course a vicar in the Church of England never really retires. Even if he gives up his parish, he still has the right to continue to be a minister. I've heard some clergy wives say that their husbands are even busier in retirement than they were before, helping out in numerous places, but James hopes to spend more time with his beloved orchids and studying snakes. He even talks of writing a book about the snakes of Ceylon.'

De Silva shuddered at the thought of snakes. He had temporarily forgotten that Reverend Peters was so interested in them, but now he recalled how useful the vicar's knowledge had been in a previous case. All the same, it seemed to him a strange passion. All he wanted to know about snakes was that they were a long way away from wherever he was.

They sipped lemonade as de Silva told Mrs Peters about his and Jane's stay at the monastery. He was careful, however, to omit any mention of the manuscript. On the way from Sunnybank, he had decided that it would be best to speak to the vicar first and gauge how he reacted to the story. If Mrs Peters was curious as to the reason for his visit to the vicarage, she was too discreet to ask. Twenty minutes later, he heard a car arrive.

'Ah, that must be my husband now,' said Mrs Peters. 'Shall we go inside? I expect your business is confidential. You can talk in private in his study.'

* * *

The study, with its dark panelling and numerous bookshelves, was pleasantly cool. Muted light came through the windows; de Silva recalled thinking on a previous visit that the room must face north. It was as cluttered as he remembered, the bookshelves crammed with leather-bound volumes, many of them with spines so faded the titles were hard to read. The musty, earthy smell of old books mingled with the aroma of the peppermints to which the vicar was partial. His desk was well-polished mahogany, topped with claret leather with gold-tooled edges and piled with letters and papers. Amongst them, an antique cut-glass inkwell with brass mountings stood on a walnut base. The brass was a little tarnished, but age had given the wood a very pleasing patina.

Peters led the way to the two easy chairs on either side of the fireplace. Like the desk, the mantelpiece was mahogany and on it were an antique silver snuff box and some silver-framed photographs, including one of the vicar and Mrs Peters on their wedding day. She wore a white dress with a long veil and a wreath of gardenias in her hair.

The vicar wore a dark suit and a glossy top hat and sported rather splendid mutton-chop whiskers as black as his hat. They must have been shaved off before he came to Nuala-for de Silva didn't remember them. He had only known Peters to be clean shaven. It gave greater prominence to his aquiline nose and the deep-set eyes that were now regarding de Silva inquiringly from under bushy grey eyebrows.

'I hope nothing too disastrous has occurred, Inspector. Although I imagine it must be of some significance if it has caused you to interrupt your holiday. I'll be glad to help if it's within my powers.'

'Thank you, sir.'

De Silva launched into Bhante Gunananda's story of how Bartholomew Parry had come to the monastery, how they had become friends, what he had told Gunananda about the manuscript, and his struggle to decide what to do with it. Peters listened carefully, waiting until he had finished before asking any questions.

'I appreciate that this monk Gunananda was very young when he knew Parry,' he said, 'but was there anything that made him think the man might not be in his right mind?'

'Bhante Gunananda realised that Parry was very troubled, but he hasn't suggested that he had lost his mental faculties.'

'You say Parry showed him the manuscript, so we can be certain that it wasn't simply a figment of Parry's imagination, but I find the story of its great antiquity rather hard to swallow. How can one know whether it's true?'

'I agree that seems to be a major obstacle, however, I believe experiments have been undertaken in America that involve something called radiocarbon dating.'

Peters nodded. 'I've read of them. It's a most interesting prospect which could lead to a great increase in our knowledge of the past, but my understanding is that the technique is very much in its infancy. I doubt it will be generally available yet, and it may be several years before it is. I've never heard of this man Parry. He may have been a charlatan for all we know, however I agree that when the time comes, if his claim is upheld, the manuscript will be of immense value, on account of its great age if nothing else. Very few manuscripts survive from the seventh or eighth centuries, and most of those claimed to be from that era have turned out to be forgeries. I'm afraid medieval monks were not immune to the desire to make money by feeding the public appetite for wondrous things. They often became very skilled at it and would have been able to write in earlier versions of languages, including Welsh.'

'Quite apart from the question of the age of the manuscript, what do you think of the claims made in it?'

'I'm a man of the cloth, so no doubt it won't surprise you when I say that I think what you have told me about our Lord's mother and the circumstance of His birth is a travesty. Some things are beyond human understanding, and that is one of them. I'm not even prepared to discuss it further.'

The bushy grey eyebrows drew together. De Silva hoped he hadn't overstepped the mark, but to his relief, Peters' expression softened a little. 'As to this matter of our Lord's missing years, however, there are numerous folk tales and legends that some people still believe in today. A lot of them are connected with the western part of the British Isles. The legend of King Arthur and his knights, for example, claims that they sleep beneath Glastonbury Tor, a prominent hill in in the county of Somerset, but that story is so tainted with medieval romance that I've always felt it should be discounted.'

Peters paused to take a handkerchief from his pocket and blow his nose. 'But the idea that Joseph of Arimathea visited Britain is, to my mind, a different matter. Some theologians believe that after our Lord's resurrection, Joseph and his followers may have brought Christianity, or at least a nascent form of it, to our islands. This would have been more than three hundred years earlier than St Augustine arrived from Rome to convert Britain to Christianity. These theologians suggest there was a Celtic church that followed a different path to the Roman one. Instead of staying in their monasteries, the monks would have travelled about preaching in the way that Jesus and his disciples did.'

Peters stuffed the handkerchief back in his pocket and reached for a small blue and gold tin on the table next to his chair. 'My wife says that I am addicted to these strong peppermints, but it seems to me a very harmless habit, so I continue.'

He opened the tin and held it out to de Silva who thanked him and took one. When he put it in his mouth, for a moment he felt as if someone had set fire to him, and he blinked.

'I imagine the effect is similar to that of the first curry I was given when I came to the island,' said Peters with a smile. 'Then one grows to like it, or the reverse. Fortunately, I have become very fond of curry.' He took a peppermint for himself and closed the lid of the tin.

'Where were we? Ah yes, Joseph of Arimathea. He seems to have been a most interesting man, although of course we are so far from the times he lived in that much of what can be ascertained about him has to be gleaned from a variety of sources then stitched together with informed conjecture. I understand you're a Buddhist, but I know that you come to church occasionally with your wife, so I take it you're familiar with what the Bible tells us of our Lord's crucifixion and resurrection.'

'Yes, I am Buddhist, but I know the stories.' As soon as the words were out of his mouth, de Silva felt a twinge of awkwardness. He hoped that describing anything in the Bible as a story wouldn't cause offence, but Peters' bushy eyebrows remained where they were.

'The Bible tells us that Joseph of Arimathea went to the Roman governor Pontius Pilate and asked for permission to take Jesus's body down from the cross and bury it. If Pilate granted him an audience and agreed to his request, I think it's a fair assumption that Joseph was a man of some importance. Indeed, he's referred to in the Bible and other ancient texts as a wealthy man and a noble official. He was also able to afford the expensive unguents that he used to anoint Jesus's body. The idea that he was an official in the field of mining for metals derives from folklore and legend. He is the patron saint of miners, and if we accept the connection, as Britain was rich in tin, it would have been natural for him to visit the island to trade. Tin was used for making many things and most importantly as an alloy with copper to make bronze. Bronze is a hard metal that was used to make weapons. A bronze blade will keep its edge far longer than any other metal available at the time.'

'But what about this idea that he was Jesus's uncle?'

Peters pondered for a moment. 'I believe Roman and Jewish law gave a male relation the right to ask for the body of a convicted criminal, but Pontius Pilates' acquiescence may have had as much to do with Joseph's wealth and status as with that. He was also offering Pilate what Pilate might have hoped would be a discreet conclusion to a very difficult situation.'

'Hmm, I hadn't thought of it that way, but it's a good point.'

'I expect you know the song that begins "*And did those feet in ancient times walk upon England's mountains green*". I'm not one of those who call it a hymn. William Blake, who wrote the words, was not a Christian. But putting that aside, I believe it may reflect what actually happened. I wouldn't be surprised if Jesus travelled far from his homeland in those missing years between his debates with the elders in the temple and the beginning of his ministry in

Judea. It's hard to credit that a man with his exceptional powers and destined for greatness learned everything he knew in the small community of Nazareth. The fact that Joseph of Arimathea was aware of him may indicate they were related and help to explain why he took Jesus with him on some of his visits to Britain. Joseph might have seen it as incumbent on him to take on the duties of a father.'

There was a gentle tap on the door and the vicar paused. It opened and Mrs Peters looked in.

'Tea will be ready soon. I hope you're not tiring our guest out, dear.' She smiled at de Silva. 'As you may have noticed, my husband tends to lose track of time.'

'I think he has pretty well plumbed the depths of my knowledge on the subject we've been discussing,' said Peters. He turned to de Silva. 'Was there anything else you wanted to ask me about?'

'Just one last thing, but it shouldn't take long.'

'I'll tell cook to wait a few more minutes, shall I?' asked Mrs Peters.

'Thank you.'

'So, what else can I help you with?' asked Peters when the door had closed behind his wife.

'As I said, this manuscript has been removed from its place in the monastery's library. At the outset, there were several suspects, but I've been able to eliminate most of them. The one that I'm left with is a man called Arthur Warrender who claims to be a retired vicar. However I'm not sure he's telling the truth and if not—'

Peters nodded. 'He has something to hide.'

'Yes, and he may either be the thief or know who is. I'd like to find out whether he's lying about being a vicar. Jane thought you might have a directory called *Crockfords* that would help.'

'Yes, I do.' Peters got up and went to one of the bookcases. He ran a finger over the faded spines on one of the shelves, selected a hefty tome and then brought it back to his chair and sat down with it in his lap.

'This should list everyone in holy orders whether they're retired or not.' Peters reached for the spectacles on the table beside him and perched them on the bridge of his nose. 'Let me see… Wakehurst, Walker, Walters, Wantage.' He looked up. 'No Warrenders. Does that help?'

'Very much so, thank you.'

'Good. Now, I think tea calls.'

* * *

Back at Sunnybank that evening, de Silva sat on the verandah after an excellent dinner consisting of his favourite pea and cashew curry with a variety of side dishes and plenty of hot fluffy rice. He felt it was a just reward after so many meals of dahl, but he wasn't at peace. It was hard not to worry about Jane. What if he had left her in danger? He tried to reassure himself by thinking of how sensible she always was and the fact that there were other people at the monastery who would be able to help her if needed, but what if Arthur Warrender had guessed why de Silva had left? There was little doubt in his mind now that Arthur was the man he was looking for. He remembered Belinda Wragge saying that he was always nosing about and not the nice man he appeared to be on the surface. It seemed she had been more perceptive than he had.

He shifted in his chair, earning a displeased miaow from Bella who had been curled up asleep on his lap. Billy snoozed at the top of the steps to the garden, one sleek black leg draped gracefully over the edge. Attracted by the light of the lamp that hung from the ceiling, small toffee-coloured moths fluttered against the glass, making soft ruffling sounds that mingled with the throb of night insects.

On his return from the vicarage, he had found a message from the Residence telling him that Archie had been delayed in Kandy and wouldn't be back in time to see him the following morning. Their meeting would have to wait until late afternoon, which would make it impossible for him to return to the monastery in daylight. The drive wouldn't be too much of a problem now that he was used to the road, but finding his way in the dark up the mountain from the place where he would have to leave the Morris was a different matter. Not only would it be harder to negotiate the rocky path, particularly the slippery parts, but there was also the risk of encountering a mountain leopard. He knew it made far better sense to wait until the following morning, but that meant another night of leaving Jane alone. Her voice echoed in his head, its usual firm tone telling him he worried too much. Perhaps she was right.

He looked at the empty whisky glass in his hand and wondered whether to have another; it might help him to sleep. But in the end, he decided against it. He would get off to bed and hope it would soon be morning.

CHAPTER 14

The following day at the monastery, Jane was in her bedroom tidying her hair in preparation for going to lunch when there was a knock at the door. She put down her hairbrush and went to answer it. Belinda Wragge stood outside. She usually wore summer dresses, but now she had on a more practical outfit of khaki trousers and shirt with a pair of sturdy brown shoes.

'As you see, I'm dressed for travelling,' she said in a tone of forced cheerfulness.

'Oh, Belinda, I'm so sorry you have to leave. And very sorry that you and Alec have had such bad luck.'

Belinda raised an eyebrow. 'To be honest, I don't think luck has had a lot to do with it. We should have seen this coming and tried to do something before it was too late, but there's no point crying over spilt milk.' She brightened. 'I've told Alec we have to learn from our mistakes. Anyway, he's not been very happy this last year or so. Perhaps it's a good thing that matters have come to a head.'

'That's very wise of you, my dear.'

Belinda laughed. 'I don't feel terribly wise at the moment, but we shall muddle through somehow. Madeleine has been very kind. She and I had a long talk and she suggested that Alec might be happier with a different kind of job, maybe something to do with publishing. She has a lot of contacts, and she says that if we'd like her to, she'll try to help.'

'That's good of her. Will Alec accept her offer?'

'I don't want to talk to him about it yet, but she says that doesn't matter. The offer is there, and I can come back to her at any time. Alec is still so cross and upset. I want to give him time to settle down before I broach the subject with him. When I do, I hope he'll agree. A change might be just what he needs.'

'Well, whatever you decide, I hope you'll both be happy.'

'Thank you.'

'Are you staying for lunch before you go? I was just about to go over to the dining room myself.'

Belinda shook her head. 'We have a taxi waiting for us, so we had something brought to our rooms.' She shuddered. 'Anyway, I don't think I could stand having to be polite to Arthur Warrender. I can tell he's never liked Alec and he feels sorry for me being married to him.'

Briskly, Belinda wiped a tear from her eye. 'I do love Alec, you know, and he isn't always like this.' She held out her hand. 'Well, goodbye.'

Jane took Belinda's outstretched hand. 'Goodbye and I wish you both the best of luck. I'm sure Shanti will be sorry not to have been able to say goodbye to you in person.'

'And I him. I hope he finds this manuscript. I don't know much about it, but it sounds important.'

'Belinda!' They turned and Jane saw Alec Wragge striding across the courtyard. Soma was a few paces behind him.

'We ought to be on our way.'

She bridled. 'Alec, I haven't said goodbye to Bhante Gunananda yet.'

'I've done that for you.' Alec's tone was abrupt, and she flushed slightly. He nodded to Jane. 'It was nice to meet you and your husband, Mrs de Silva.' Jane saw an unexpected flash of humour in his eyes. 'I hope you weren't too disappointed we didn't furnish the solution to your mystery after all.'

Without waiting for an answer, he took Belinda's arm and turned to where Soma was waiting at the bottom of the steps to the verandah. 'Thank you for your hospitality. It's been a memorable visit, but somehow, I don't think we'll be coming back.'

Jane and Soma watched the couple walk away to where Chatura and two other young monks waited beside their luggage. They hoisted the cases onto their shoulders and the little party set off in the direction of the downhill path.

'Some guests give us pleasure when they arrive and some when they leave,' remarked Soma dryly.

'That's not very charitable.'

'But true.'

Jane sighed. 'I don't envy poor Belinda, but she tells me that Madeleine has been very kind and offered to help Alec find a new job.'

'Yes, she's developed rather a soft spot for Belinda, and she likes to help people.'

'I'm sure she does.'

Soma gave Jane a sideways look. 'Not everyone sees that in her.' He paused. 'When do you expect Shanti back?'

'Before he left, he said he might be able to get away from Nuala today, but if he isn't here by nightfall, I expect it will be tomorrow.'

'You'll be glad to see him.'

'I will.'

Briefly, Jane's mind turned to home. Yesterday evening after supper she had thought enviously of Shanti, probably sitting on the verandah enjoying the peace of the evening with Billy and Bella for company.

'Now, don't let me keep you from your lunch,' said Soma. He chuckled. 'I expect you're looking forward to our dahl.'

'Of course.'

Jane was about to part from him when she noticed a man she didn't recognise over by the steps to the main hall.

She put up a hand to shade her eyes. 'Is that a new guest?'

Soma glanced in the direction towards which she was looking. 'Yes, his name's James Vine. He's been hiking in the hills and became confused about his way. He was very relieved when he came across the monastery. He intends to rest here for a night or two before travelling on. It's fortunate that the Wragges' rooms are now available.'

CHAPTER 15

De Silva had woken early that morning, surprised for a moment that he was alone, then he remembered that he had left Jane up at the monastery. He climbed out of bed, found his dressing gown and slippers, and put them on. He had only just reached the drawing room when Billy and Bella joined him. 'I doubt any guard dog would be more efficient than you two,' he remarked as he opened the door. He watched them scoot across the verandah, down the steps, and into the bushes.

The temperature was pleasant, so he went outside too and sat down in one of the garden chairs to watch the sun come up. He wondered if Jane was also up enjoying the sunrise.

'Good morning, sahib.'

Their servant Delisha had come out of the house. 'Shall I tell cook to serve your breakfast soon, sahib?'

De Silva thought for a moment. He wasn't due to see Archie until the afternoon and there was nothing he needed to do before that except drop into the station to see if Prasanna and Nadar were behaving themselves. 'I'll have a bath first,' he said. 'Tell cook there's no need to rush.'

Just then Billy and Bella reappeared and trotted over to Delisha, wrapping themselves around her legs. De Silva grinned. 'I think some are in a hurry though.'

'They're hungry now,' said Delisha with a smile. 'Whilst

you and the memsahib have been away, they haven't wanted to eat so much. Cook prepared chicken and rice for them but they only ate a little.'

De Silva felt a pang of guilt. Still, with the information Reverend Peters had provided, he felt confident that he and Jane wouldn't need to stay away much longer.

After Delisha departed to feed the cats, he fell to thinking about how he would approach matters when he returned to the monastery. First, he must tell Bhante Gunananda and Soma what he had discovered about Arthur Warrender. After that, it would be time to challenge the fellow. An unwelcome thought occurred to him that Arthur might already have managed to smuggle the manuscript out of the monastery. Those plant-hunting excursions would afford a convenient cover. If that were the case, he thought gloomily, and Arthur wouldn't cooperate, it was going to make life very difficult.

* * *

He sat down to breakfast with a sigh of pleasure at the sight of the plate of egg hoppers that Leela put in front of him. They were accompanied by a tasty vegetable curry and a fiery coconut sambol that tickled his taste buds very pleasingly. As he ate, he thought guiltily of Jane who was no doubt faced with yet another breakfast of dahl. He didn't want to offend their hosts, but perhaps he could discreetly take back a few snacks for her to vary the monotony of the monastery's food.

'Please tell cook that I'd like some of the spicy lentil patties and fried cashews that the memsahib likes, to take with me when I go back to the monastery tomorrow,' he said to Leela when she brought in some fresh tea. 'Oh, and some milk toffee would be nice too.'

Leela nodded. 'And will you be wanting dinner tonight, sahib?' she asked as she poured the tea.

'Yes, please. I'm happy for cook to choose the menu.'

When he had finished breakfast, he went to take a look at Jane's car before he left for the station. He was pleased to see that it was spotlessly clean and in good condition.

At the station, Prasanna and Nadar jumped to their feet when he walked in, chorusing a good morning.

'How have things been here?'

'Very quiet, sir,' said Prasanna.

'I wish I could say the same of my holiday.' He told them about the events at the monastery.

'Should one of us come back with you, sir?' asked Prasanna when he had finished. 'In case you need help?'

'Hmm. That's probably a good idea. I'll take you, Prasanna. Nadar, you can be in charge here.'

Nadar's chest seemed to swell a little. 'Yes, sir.'

'I'm seeing Mr Clutterbuck this afternoon. After that I'll go straight home. I'll pick you up from here tomorrow morning, Prasanna. You'd better let Kuveni know that you may be away for a couple of days. And bring some warm clothes with you. It gets chilly up at the monastery at night.' He chuckled. 'I hope you like dahl.'

Prasanna looked perplexed. 'Dahl, sir? Why wouldn't I?'

'The monastery doesn't provide much else by way of food. I suggest you ask Kuveni to give you a good meal before we go and pack you up one or two of your favourite snacks to bring with you.'

* * *

It was much busier up at the Residence than it had been at the police station. As he passed the secretaries' office on his way to Archie's study, de Silva heard a brisk tapping of keys.

A greater number of junior officials with files tucked under their arms or letters in their hands were in evidence than usual. Wryly, de Silva wondered if Archie's staff were keen to show that they had not been idle in their boss's absence.

When he went into Archie's study, de Silva received an ecstatic welcome from Lady, the Labrador.

Archie grinned. 'You'll have to watch out, de Silva. Those cats of yours will be jealous if they smell dog on you. Now, what's this all about? I thought you were on holiday.'

He listened whilst de Silva gave an account of events at the monastery. 'I agree it's advisable for you to go back there and try to sort things out,' he said when de Silva had finished, 'and you have my authority to do so. A theft is a theft, although as to the purported contents of this manuscript, this business about the Virgin Mary seems to me to be nothing more than meddling speculation.'

'Reverend Peters said much the same.'

'Sound man, Peters. Still, if the wrong people get their hands on something, one doesn't know where it will end, so it's important to make sure that doesn't happen. Had Peters heard of this fellow Parry these monks told you about?'

'No, but he agreed that if it were possible for the manuscript to be examined in the future and its antiquity confirmed, it would be of immense value, independent of its contents.'

'I expect he's right about that.' Archie rolled his shoulders and heaved a sigh. 'Very hard chairs at the Kandy Residence and too much time sitting in them. I need a good walk to limber me up.'

He bent down to pat Lady who had raised her head from her paws at the mention of a walk and was starting to scramble up. 'Not yet, girl. Go on, de Silva. What did Peters have to say about this business of Jesus coming to England?'

'He was of the opinion that there may be some truth in it.'

'I think there might be too. There's that hymn for a start. The one about building Jerusalem in England's green and pleasant land. I expect you know it, stirring stuff. I believe William Blake who wrote the poem was a visionary, not a man of the cloth, but I spent my boyhood in that part of the world, and I recall that there are legends and folktales too. It seems fair to assume the claim's not just pure fantasy.'

He removed his hand from Lady's head, and she settled down again, but her chestnut eyes remained open, gazing soulfully in the direction of the door to the garden.

'Interesting point about Joseph of Arimathea being involved in the tin trade. I believe he's the patron saint of miners and metal workers which suggests that could be true. When I was a lad, I remember my father taking me to see the casting of a new bell for our local church. He was a country solicitor and a big wheel in the parish. The old bell had cracked, and he'd taken it on himself to have the replacement made. Watching the casting was an extraordinary experience – the heat, the flames, the roar of the furnace, and the molten metal flowing red like a river out of Hades. I heard one of the workmen muttering something under his breath that sounded like "Joseph was a tin man". Afterwards when I asked my father what that was about, he just laughed and said local folk were very superstitious, but much later on, I heard that metalworkers often used the phrase for luck when they were casting something. A kind of talisman, I suppose.'

Archie fell silent, perhaps dwelling on times past. De Silva tried to imagine him as a boy, interested in folktales and legends, but without much success.

'It was a very long time ago,' said Archie, rousing himself. He stood up, swiftly followed by Lady. 'Time for that walk. I expect you want to be on your way, de Silva. I look forward to hearing how you get on.'

CHAPTER 16

The following morning, used to the mountain road by now, de Silva drove faster than he had on his first journey, and he and Prasanna reached the place where they had to leave the Morris in plenty of time to walk to the monastery in daylight. There were no monks to help with the rest of the climb, but de Silva was reasonably confident that he knew the way and Prasanna only carried a small bag.

They walked briskly at first but then de Silva was surprised to find Prasanna lagging behind.

'Any problem, Sergeant? Stone in your shoe?'

'Sorry, sir. It's just I've never been anywhere like this before. It's all so…so…*different*.'

'Yes, not at all like the countryside around Nuala and Hatton. I think living up here all the time wouldn't suit me, but there are some wonderful sights. You haven't seen all of them yet.'

They reached the grassy plateau, and the rest of the mountain came into view. Even though the sky was a forget-me-not blue, witches' fingers of cloud still clawed at the trees on the upper slopes, eventually coalescing to hide the summit.

'I've not seen the mountain top once in all the time we've been here,' remarked de Silva. He rolled his shoulders. 'On we go. Nearly there, you may be pleased to hear.'

A few minutes later they passed through the gate and

into the courtyard. There was no one about. 'The monks are probably in their quarters,' said de Silva. 'I don't think we'll approach Arthur Warrender straight away. First, I'd better let Mrs de Silva and Bhante Soma know that I'm back. They might have something new to tell me.'

Prasanna looked in the direction of the guest quarters. 'That's Mrs de Silva coming now, sir.'

'Excellent.'

They went over to greet Jane but when she was close enough for de Silva to see the expression on her face, he realised immediately that something was wrong.

'What's happened?' he asked.

'Shanti, I'm so glad you're back. It's Arthur Warrender. He was found dead in his quarters early this morning.'

* * *

'It was Anzan who found him,' said Jane when the three of them were in the de Silvas' sitting room. 'When he took Arthur his washing water this morning, there he was, lying on the floor by the fireplace. He looked to have fallen against it and hit his head hard. There was an awful lot of blood. Poor Anzan is still very upset.'

'Were there any other marks on the body?'

'Soma and the infirmarian examined it and didn't find any, but it's clear that someone had searched the room. There are papers on the floor and clothes pulled out of drawers.'

'Someone looking for the manuscript, I imagine. They'd hardly be after Arthur's notes on plants. Was there anything else?'

'A chair overturned close to the fireplace. I suppose he might have stumbled on that and fallen.'

'Where's the body now?'

'I managed to stop Soma from having it removed,

although it was difficult. He's keen to have it cremated as soon as possible on health grounds.'

'That's understandable, but I can't allow it. I'll have to arrange for it to be taken down to Nuala as soon as possible. There will need to be an autopsy to establish the precise cause of death. I suppose no one heard anything. The sound of a fall? A cry for help?'

'I'm afraid not, so we're not sure exactly what time it happened. After Arthur left us when we'd finished dinner, Madeleine and I stayed on in the dining room for a long time, talking about all kinds of things, but if it was after we'd returned to our quarters, we must have been fast asleep.' Jane gave an involuntary shiver. 'It's horrible to think I might have been close by and did nothing.'

'You mustn't blame yourself.'

'I know, but it's difficult not to feel guilty. Even though Madeleine didn't much like him, she's distressed too. She's in her quarters now. Do you want to speak to her?'

'I don't think I need trouble her at the moment. If it's necessary, I'll visit her later, but I want to talk to Soma.'

* * *

'As far as I'm aware, all the monks went to their quarters as usual after prayers,' said Soma. 'They didn't leave them again until early morning when it was time to go out to collect alms.'

They sat at the table in the dining room, Prasanna a little apart from de Silva, Jane, and Soma, with a notebook in front of him in which he was assiduously jotting down what was being said. Outside, dusk was swiftly gathering so the light in the room came from the single oil lamp on the table. Its sickly light threw their shadows onto the walls and left pockets of darkness in the corners of the room. Instinctively, no one had taken Arthur's old chair.

'Are you sure none of them came out earlier?' asked de Silva.

'I've questioned them all and they say not. I doubt they would lie to me.'

'The thing is,' said Jane, 'after you went back to Nuala, someone new came to the monastery. He took the Wragges' rooms.'

'Ah, now we're getting somewhere. Is he still here?'

'No, we're not sure when he left, but no one's seen him since Arthur's body was found.'

'He gave his name as James Vine,' said Soma. 'He told us he'd been hiking in the hills and lost his way. He made a big point of how relieved he was to find the monastery and how grateful he was for our offer of hospitality.'

'I suppose it might be a coincidence, but the timing is suspicious. Are you sure he came on foot?'

'That's what he said.'

'If it's true, hopefully he hasn't gone far, but we only have his word for it that he didn't have a vehicle. What did he look like?'

'I'm afraid I just saw him briefly from across the court-yard,' said Jane. 'I was in the garden, and he was at the bottom of the steps to the prayer hall. He was dressed for hiking in khaki trousers and shirt with a broad-brimmed hat and sturdy boots, but I wasn't close enough to see his face and I can't tell you the colour of his hair because he didn't remove the hat before he went inside. Did you get a better look at him, Soma?'

'We spoke briefly after he arrived, and I arranged for him to take the rooms that the Wragges had vacated, but I'm afraid I didn't take much notice of his looks, so I can't add to your description except to say that he had grey hair that obviously hadn't been cut for a while.'

'Did he have much with him?' asked de Silva.

'Only a small rucksack.'

That seemed rather improvident, thought de Silva. And Vine had also claimed to have lost his way. He didn't sound like a seasoned hiker. 'Do you know if he and Arthur met?' he asked.

'I'm afraid I don't. I'll ask if anyone saw them together, but as far as I'm aware, Vine wanted to keep to himself. He asked for his meals to be served in his rooms.'

'I see. Well, if anyone can give a more detailed description, it would be helpful.'

Soma stood up. 'I'll get on with that now, shall I?'

There was something abrupt in his tone that surprised de Silva. He wondered if Soma was feeling criticised for admitting Vine into the monastery without questioning his story.

'Perhaps he should have done,' said Jane when Soma had left, and de Silva mentioned it to her. 'Maybe I should have suggested that he did.'

'Of course, hindsight is a great advantage,' said de Silva kindly. 'Did you notice any alteration in Arthur's behaviour after Vine arrived?'

Jane pondered for a moment. 'At dinner last night he was much quieter than usual. Might it mean he knew Vine had come and was worried about it?'

'I think it's time we took a look at their respective quarters. You'd better come too, Sergeant.'

* * *

He would never be impervious to the smell of death, thought de Silva as he surveyed the room where Arthur had met his end. He sent Prasanna to search the washroom and bedroom then crouched beside Arthur's body and pulled back the sheet that covered it. Jane was right, there was a lot of blood. Arthur had bled profusely from the gash at the back of his head. His hair, shirt and jacket were crusted with blood and the fireplace, and the surrounding floor were liberally splattered with it.

Prasanna returned and de Silva stood up. 'Anything to report?'

'Nothing out of the ordinary, sir.'

De Silva looked down at Arthur's body. 'Not a pretty sight, eh?'

'No, sir. Shall I cover him up again?'

'Yes, do that.' De Silva was glad to see that Prasanna seemed to be coping well with the gruesome situation. He left him to make a thorough search of the sitting room and went next door to the Wragges' old quarters to find Jane.

'Vine doesn't seem to have left much of an impression,' she said. 'There's nothing in the bedroom and washroom and not a lot here.' She indicated a half-finished bowl of congealed dahl, an empty glass, and a newspaper opened at the crossword page with a stub of pencil beside it. De Silva glanced at the date of the newspaper. It was several days old and wasn't much help. There were various places, including Nuala, where he might have bought it.

'Vine could be anywhere by now,' he said. 'We need to send out alerts in case anyone spots him. I'm not sure Oyagama has any telephones, so we may have to go further on to...'

He stopped. Oyagama – a man with grey hair had arrived in a Land Rover and gone into the hotel. He remembered thinking then that he looked familiar. Now it came to him that he was the man he'd previously seen in Manil's bar in Nuala, and from Soma's description, scanty as it was, he might also be the one who had come to the monastery. Why claim he was a hiker when he had a perfectly good means of motor transport at his disposal?

'What is it, Shanti?' asked Jane.

'James Vine. I'm wondering if that's really his name.

Because I've seen someone before who might answer to the description Soma gave me. Twice in fact. Once in Oyagama, driving a Land Rover, and before that at Manil's bar in Nuala.'

'Was he using a different name?'

'I don't know what name he used when he was in Manil's, but a young lad I asked at Oyagama told me his name was Jim Aevens.'

Jane's brow furrowed and she was silent for a moment.

'Have you had an idea?' asked de Silva.

'Just give me a moment.'

After a brief pause, she picked up the pencil beside the newspaper and jotted down the letters in Vine's name in the blank space beside the crossword. 'I think I've worked it out. Do you see? When I rearrange the letters like this,' she wrote them down again but in a different order, 'they spell Jim Aevens. It's an anagram. Vine is probably a crossword fan, as am I.'

De Silva stared at the two names. 'You're right, they do, and I remember he was doing a crossword when I saw him in Manil's bar, but I'm afraid it will take a bit more than that to nail him.'

'But it's a start, isn't it?'

'It is, but before we raise the alert, let's check the parking area for any evidence that the Land Rover I saw him driving in Oyagama was there.'

* * *

At the parking area, the Morris was the only car in sight.

'There are no tyre tracks,' said Jane, 'but as the ground's so dry, it isn't very likely there would be, so the car might have been here.'

Prasanna returned from searching the area's perimeter.

167

'I think I've found something, sir.'

He pointed to a gap in the trees. De Silva went over to it with him; on the far side there was an apron of flat land that would be large enough to accommodate a Land Rover. It was strewn with numerous branches of palm and other trees.

De Silva lifted up one of them. 'This isn't heavy so I doubt it would have fallen because of its own weight. Anyway, the end's been cleanly cut.' He ran his thumb over the severed end. 'There's still some sap here.' He examined another branch, and it was in the same condition. 'These branches have been cut down recently. Well done for spotting the gap, Prasanna. It's an old trick, isn't it? Vine will have used the branches to hide his Land Rover, then discarded them when he left. There's only one place he could drive to from here that's immediately at the bottom of the mountain and that's Oyagama. We'll start there.'

'Shall I go back to the monastery?' asked Jane. 'It will be quite a squash for the three of us in the Morris.'

'If you're sure you'll be alright.'

'Of course I will.'

'I'll come back for you as soon as I can.'

CHAPTER 17

'Vine's real name is Aevens,' said de Silva when he returned to the monastery two days later to collect Jane. 'His car was found broken down and abandoned near Nuala yesterday. I had it towed to Gopallawa's garage, and they'll keep it there. Amongst the items we found in the boot, there was a hatchet. Just the thing for hacking off tree branches. I sent out alerts to all the nearby railway stations and we were lucky. Aevens was apprehended as he boarded the train from Nanu Oya to Peradeniya. I'm afraid, however, that there's no sign of the manuscript.'

'Oh dear.'

'Aevens admits that he and Arthur planned for Arthur to steal it. Aevens' job was to find a buyer. He's a dealer in antiquities and has a respectable front for his business, but my guess is this isn't the only shady activity he's engaged in behind it. In the course of his work, he'd come across references to the manuscript and an indication that it was at one time in Bartholomew Parry's possession. He managed to track down Parry's obituary in an old newspaper and it mentioned that Parry spent the last years of his life at the monastery. Aevens reasoned that if Parry brought the manuscript with him, it might still be here.'

'So what connected Aevens to Arthur?'

'They met a few years ago when Arthur was trying to sell what he claimed were some Roman artefacts that he'd found. As we learned from Reverend Peters, Arthur was never in the church. He taught in various minor public schools, but he was at one time a lay preacher which gave him the idea of posing as a clergyman. He also had an interest in antiquities. Aevens told him the artefacts weren't genuine, but suggested he keep in touch in case he found anything else. Arthur did contact him from time to time and Aevens was aware that he was short of money. He agreed he'd be the one to come to the monastery, and if he could find the manuscript, he'd steal it.'

'Does Aevens say Arthur didn't find it?'

'Arthur claimed he hadn't been able to, but Aevens suspected he was lying, hoping to keep it for himself. Aevens didn't deny he and Arthur argued. He swore, however, that Arthur was alive and well when he left him, and that he left him empty handed. Beyond that, he refused to say anything more.'

'Do you believe him?'

'I find it difficult to. To my mind there are three possibilities. It could be that in the course of their argument, Aevens pushed or struck Arthur, and Arthur fell, hitting his head.'

'And the second?'

'Aevens didn't touch Arthur, but he alarmed him so much that Arthur recoiled, stumbled, and fell. In both cases, Aevens then decided to make a run for it. The third possibility is that Arthur was alive when Aevens left as he claims, but Arthur was probably very shaken. He may have sat down in that chair we saw overturned on the floor. When he stood up, he lost his balance and fell. In that case, his death would have been purely accidental and Aevens would be an innocent man.'

'So what happens now?'

'I've reported to Archie. It will be up to him to take it from here. He'll consult with William Petrie. In view of the seriousness of the matter, as Petrie's the government agent and Archie's boss, Archie considers it only proper for him to be involved, and I agree.'

'I still feel so guilty that I heard nothing that night,' said Jane. 'Have you spoken to Soma and Gunananda yet?'

'Only Soma. He met me as I arrived.'

'How did he take the news?'

'He said he was glad Aevens had been arrested, and pleased when I told him that Arthur's body will be taken down to Kandy tomorrow. But he didn't say anything about the manuscript or seem interested when I promised that efforts will still be made to find it. To be honest, I'm not sure yet what, if anything, can be done, but I suppose it's not beyond the bounds of possibility that it will turn up one day. I think in view of what it may contain, plenty of people would prefer it to be under lock and key.'

'What do we do next?'

'I want to see Arthur's body safely dispatched, but after that I don't think there's anything more that we can accomplish here. I told Soma we'll probably leave tomorrow.'

'Then I'll pack up after supper. We must say our goodbyes. Oh, and poor Anzan. Will you speak to Gunananda and Soma as you promised? With everything that's gone on, I expect it slipped your mind.'

'I'm glad you reminded me. Let's talk to them in the morning when we go to say goodbye.'

Jane looked up at the sky. It was a beautiful blue with only a few puffs of cloud drifting across it.

'It would be nice to take a last walk up to the lake. I've visited it several times whilst I've been on my own here, and I don't suppose we'll be back for a long time, if at all.'

'Good idea, I'll come with you. It will still be light for a couple of hours. I'll tell Prasanna to stay here and keep an eye on the body. I brought a few snacks from home that I thought you might like as a change from dahl. With all the excitement, the hamper's still in the car, but hopefully some of the contents will still be edible, so I'll fetch that too. Maybe we can have a little picnic at the lake.'

'That's a lovely idea. I'll go and change my shoes.'

* * *

De Silva was pleased to find that, even encumbered by the hamper of snacks, he accomplished the walk to the lake with considerably less difficulty than he had that first time. All this walking and the monastery's plain diet had some benefits. For once the top of the mountain was visible, standing out in all its glory against the clear sky.

He and Jane sat down on a rock, and Jane opened the hamper and looked inside. 'Fried cashew nuts! How lovely.'

'I'm afraid the lentil patties have suffered from their protracted stay in the car,' said de Silva ruefully. 'But I think the milk toffee will be fine, if a bit soggier than it should be.'

'I hope you gave something to Prasanna.'

'Kuveni prepared a few snacks for him before we left Nuala.'

'Good.'

For a while they sat in companionable silence, eating the toffee and munching the cashew nuts as they admired the lake's sparkling waters and its magnificent setting. He remembered the first time he'd seen it and the fun that the monks had been having. Life in the monastery demanded discipline and dedication, but he was glad there was also time for simple pleasures.

'I wonder where the manuscript is now?' mused Jane, shading her eyes from the sun as she gazed at the view. 'Do you think that what it contains really has the power to overturn what the gospels tell us about Mary?'

'I've no idea, my love. It may contain nothing more than

stories distorted by time. After all, if it's as old as Parry thought, hundreds of years had already passed since the time of Jesus.'

'It's astonishing to think that something like that lay neglected in the monastery's library for so many years. Remind me, did Gunananda say that Parry ever told him how it came into his possession?'

'No, perhaps the whole story will never be uncovered.' He stood up, dusting traces of the spicy coating on the cashew nuts off his palms. 'I suppose we ought to go down before the light fades.' He grinned. 'One last dinner, then tomorrow evening we'll be at home.'

'Will you be glad?'

'Of course, won't you?'

'In many ways, and of course I've missed everyone, but I wish we weren't leaving loose ends here.'

De Silva shrugged. 'I know what you mean, but perhaps that will have to be the case.' He took her hand and helped her to her feet. 'Shall we pack up and go down? I expect a feast of dahl awaits.'

CHAPTER 18

'Bhante Gunananda is too unwell to leave his bed,' said Soma when he came to see de Silva and Jane the following morning. 'He's sent me in his place and hopes you will forgive him for not coming himself.'

'Please tell him that we understand and we're not the slightest bit offended,' replied Jane. 'We're only sorry not to say goodbye in person. We hope he feels better soon, don't we, Shanti?'

De Silva nodded.

'You're very kind.' Soma gave them a strained smile. De Silva waited. It wasn't hard to detect that the monk had something to tell them that he was finding difficult to express.

'Bhante Gunananda and I have agreed that we can't let you go without telling you what we feel you have a right to know,' Soma continued. 'I doubt it will please you, but there it is. You mentioned that the search for the manuscript will continue. We're grateful for your offer, but it won't be necessary.'

'I suspect a decision to give up the search won't be left in my hands,' said de Silva cautiously. He thought back to his conversation with Soma the previous day, and Soma's apparent indifference to the fate of the manuscript. Was he about to reveal that he was the thief after all?

The monk seemed to read his mind. 'No,' he said quickly,

'when Madeleine and I told you we had nothing to do with the theft, it was the truth. It isn't necessary for anyone to continue looking for the manuscript because we already know what's happened to it. I'm afraid Bhante Gunananda is responsible for its disappearance.'

'What! But why?' asked Jane.

'After everything that's taken place, I think no one could blame him more than he does himself. I blame myself too. If I hadn't been so quick to ask for help when I thought the manuscript had been stolen, he might eventually have confessed to me that, believing he hasn't long to live, he destroyed it himself. Of course, he knew where to find it and where the librarian kept the key to the cupboard. No one would be surprised to see Bhante Gunananda enter the prayer hall. He chose a time when it was quiet, went quickly to the library, and removed the manuscript from its box. After that he took it to his quarters where he tore it into small pieces and carefully burned each one.'

De Silva thought of the brass bowl he had noticed on his first visit to Bhante Gunananda. He had assumed the large amount of ash in it came from incense, but perhaps there had been more to it than that.

'It's likely no one would ever have realised the manuscript was missing,' Soma went on, 'had it not been for the fact that whilst he was in the library, Bhante Gunananda was startled by a noise in the prayer hall. Afraid he would be discovered with the cupboard still open and the manuscript in his hands, he accidentally put the box back in a different place to the one in which he found it. Unfortunately for him, the librarian has sharp eyes and a good memory.'

'But why did he want to destroy the manuscript?' asked Jane.

Soma sighed. 'I admit it wasn't easy for me to hear his reason. I'm afraid he thought I might be tempted to make money by selling it after he was gone. He's apologised for his lack of trust in me. I hope we understand each other better now.'

'When did you first learn about this?' asked de Silva.

'Bhante Gunananda told me after Arthur Warrender's body was found. He didn't want anyone else to suffer for his actions. Warrender's death is a burden we shall both have to live with.'

'You were not to blame,' said Jane gently. 'Neither of you could be expected to know what would happen.'

'It's good of you to say so. Your visit has turned out rather differently from what you might have anticipated, hasn't it? I hope you'll remember the good parts as well as the bad.'

'Of course we will,' said Jane.

'If there's anything we can do to make amends—'

'There is one thing. Shall I explain about Anzan, Shanti?' De Silva nodded. 'Please do.'

CHAPTER 19

Three months later

It was a Saturday morning, and de Silva and Jane sat on the verandah drinking their mid-morning tea. The previous month, de Silva had been called down to Colombo to give evidence in Jim Aevens's trial. Aevens had been convicted of manslaughter. He was spared a conviction for murder after the autopsy confirmed that Arthur Warrender's death had been caused by the blow to his head which might have been the result of an accident.

Jane had stayed in touch with Madeleine from whom she had received the sad, but not unexpected, news of Bhante Gunananda's death. Madeleine sent happier news of Anzan. Soma, who was now in charge at the monastery, had talked to him about his predicament and subsequently interceded with his family on his behalf. Soma had managed to convince them that their son was not cut out for a monastic life. He was now working as a carpenter in Oyagama and plans for his marriage to his girlfriend were well advanced.

Leela appeared at the door to the drawing room. 'The post has arrived, memsahib. Shall I bring it out to you?'

'Yes, please.'

'The postman's late this morning,' remarked de Silva as Leela went back inside. She returned with an envelope addressed to de Silva that to his displeasure looked like a bill, and a parcel for the two of them.

'Were we expecting something?' he asked.

'I don't think so.' Jane undid the brown paper wrapping. 'Why, it's a book. A book by Charles Castlemaine, no less.'

She opened the letter that had come with it inside the parcel and began to read. 'It's from Madeleine. The book has just been published and she thought we might like a copy. Soma asked her to send his best wishes and hopes we enjoy it.'

She continued with the letter then smiled. 'Madeleine writes that they added two characters before the book went to the publishers: a Sinhalese policeman and his English wife. Apparently, they play an important role in the story. She and Soma hope we approve.'

De Silva chuckled. 'When you reply, you must tell her that we're delighted, at least I am. It's not every day that one finds oneself in a book. One might call it a novel experience.' He glanced at Jane's expression. 'Have I no chance of making a success as a comedian?'

She raised an eyebrow. 'I'm afraid not, dear. The police force is definitely the best place for you.'

* * * *

AUTHOR'S NOTE

Thank you for reading this book. Bartholomew Parry and his manuscript are, of course, figments of my imagination, and the idea for the story was derived from numerous sources. I appreciate there may be readers who have strong objections to some if not all of the theories these sources put forward, and I in no way endorse them, but I'm grateful that they sparked off the idea for a new adventure for Shanti and Jane. Hopefully, they will be of interest to others, even those who disagree with them, and if you would like to know more, please read on.

Much has been written about the theory that Joseph of Arimathea was a wealthy trader in metals and visited Britain on numerous occasions, spending time in Cornwall, which was particularly rich in tin, and in Somerset where lead and silver were mined. These commodities were of immense value in the ancient world, tin in particular since it was used as an alloy with copper to make bronze, the much harder metal that was suitable for weaponry. It was also an important metal in the Romans' famous plumbing systems and used to plate everyday utensils to avoid the risk of poisoning if they were made of copper, as was common.

It has also been claimed that some if not all of Jesus's missing years between the ages of twelve and thirty were also spent in Britain, namely Cornwall and Somerset in the west of the country. West Country folklore is very specific, claiming that he came by ship with Joseph of Arimathea on trading missions. They landed on the Cornish coast then eventually moved northwards. After crossing the Quantock Hills, they reached Bridgewater in Somerset where they boarded a punt and crossed the lakes and marshes that covered the area at the time to the foot of the Mendip Hills, ending their journey high up at a place that still exists called Priddy. There Jesus stayed for a considerable time, talking and working with the local miners before returning to Nazareth. The visit gave rise to the old expression, "As sure as our Lord was in Priddy."

It stands to reason that Jesus must have lived somewhere in his missing years leading up to the commencement of his ministry. If he had remained in Nazareth or its environs, wouldn't his presence have attracted more attention? It's hard to believe that the twelve-year-old boy who astonished the temple elders with his precocious intellectual powers when he disputed with them in Jerusalem simply faded into obscurity. St Luke's gospel tells us that after the episode in the temple, Jesus came to Nazareth with his parents and lived under their authority, "increasing in stature with God and man" but that doesn't seem to amount to much of a build-up for the charismatic preacher and miracle worker who burst upon the scene some eighteen years later. Interestingly, Luke also wrote that Jesus offended the people of Nazareth when he stood up to preach to them at that time and they seemed only vaguely to remember who he was.

So, do the gospels tell the full story of Jesus's missing years, and if not, where was he? Why would Britain, a damp misty island on the edge of the Mediterranean world, be the place where he chose to live? One reason may have been that Britain was notable for remaining independent of the Romans. The islanders had fought off Julius Caesar and his armies in 55 and 54 BC and were only conquered long after

Jesus's death in 43 AD. A young man coming from Judea, which had been subjugated by the Romans, might have regarded Britain as a beacon of independence. It might also have been the place where one who was making a name for himself as a radical orator and religious teacher would be safe from Roman scrutiny and persecution until he was ready to return to his homeland.

A further reason may have concerned the Druids. These mysterious priests of Ancient Britain had been known of for centuries. The Greek writer Strabo writes that they were greatly respected and considered very learned and wise. They were entrusted with important decisions at both a private and public level, and simply by their presence were reputed to have the power to halt battles and draw down the starlight. Their headquarters at Stonehenge, the famous circle of gigantic standing stones, was at the time one of the largest structures in the world. Such tales may have aroused Jesus's curiosity and a desire to see these priests for himself and learn more about them.

Going back to Priddy, an interesting find was made there that also has a bearing on the story of Jesus in Britain. The area is known for its swallets, deep sinkholes that are today thought to have been caused by seismic activity or the collapse of abandoned mine works. In the 1970s some of these swallets were explored, and a variety of items found, including ancient beakers and the bones of men and animals that appeared to have been dismembered with knives. Getting down into these swallets is challenging now and must have been even more so in ancient times. Might the effort involved in overcoming the difficulties faced by whoever left the items behind be explained by the swallets being used for some important ritual purpose, possibly connected to the mythical Underworld? In his book *The Missing Years of Jesus*, Dennis Price suggests there may be a link to the presence of Jesus in Priddy. In the ancient Graeco-Roman world, belief in the Underworld was common, and there are stories that the gates to it were located at a variety of places. Price takes the view that the story of Jesus visiting Priddy may have been conflated with these stories, giving rise to the medieval legend of the Harrowing of Hell, in which Jesus was reputed to have descended into the Underworld after the Resurrection, bringing back some of the souls of the dead, including those of Adam and Eve.

Last but not least, if it is true that Joseph of Arimathea came to Britain, perhaps even on a fairly regular basis, Jesus would have had the all-important means of getting here. The voyage would have been a difficult and risky one. Dennis Price points to the story of Jesus sleeping through a terrible storm whilst his disciples remained awake and terrified. Does the story indicate that he was a seasoned sailor, used to travelling with Joseph and untroubled by rough weather at sea?

The Virgin Birth is a far more controversial topic than theories about Jesus's missing years. In the time when this story is set, most Christians would have found denial of it abhorrent.

In *The Almighty King*, Einon Johns argues that Jesus's father was actually a mortal man, possibly a British prince. He bases his argument on a claim that during the customary period of betrothal to Jesus's earthly father Joseph, a descendant of King David, Mary accompanied Joseph of Arimathea, who was her uncle, to Britain. There he may have encouraged her union with a British prince in the hope of uniting the royal families of Britain and Judea to throw off the Roman yoke. Johns further speculates that when Mary returned to Judea, she was pregnant. Was the Virgin Birth a convenient fiction invented by Joseph of Arimathea to persuade Joseph to accept Mary and marry her, but not consummate the marriage until after Jesus was born, appearing to fulfil the biblical prophecy that the

Messiah would be born of a virgin? However, Johns has nothing to offer to back up his theories apart from circumstantial evidence.

A Complicated Pregnancy, by the American theologian Kyle Roberts, delves much deeper into the question of the Virgin Birth and may be of interest to some readers. Roberts poses the idea that even if Jesus was the product of a regular mortal union and able to experience all the emotions and suffering of an ordinary person, it wouldn't prevent him from also being fully divine and charged by God with saving the world. In fact, he argues, accepting a mortal birth for Jesus may lead to a richer view of religion, focusing more on tolerance and humanity and less on what he describes as "doctrinal gatekeeping". Unlike the Resurrection, he writes, the Virgin Birth doesn't need to be an essential element of Christian belief. He notes that neither of the accounts of Jesus's life given by Saint John, Saint Mark, and Saint Paul mention it. Why would they ignore such an astonishing event?

It is beyond the scope of this note to cover everything in Roberts' book; however if he's right, it begs the question of why the story of the Virgin Birth came about. He has two suggestions.

One is that there may have been a feeling that an extraordinary person like Jesus needed an extraordinary birth. There are plenty of instances of this in the ancient world, for example Alexander the Great was believed by many, including himself, to be the son of Zeus, who allegedly came to his mother Olympias in the form of a thunderbolt on the eve of her wedding to King Philip of Macedon. The other suggestion is that Jesus's birth was the result of premarital sex, to which Mary may or may not have consented, a situation that would have been severely disapproved of and probably punished. Whatever the truth, Roberts' book makes for a thought-provoking read, combining deep religious faith with a lightness of touch.

BIBLIOGRAPHY

The Almighty King by Einon Johns
(Kindle edition – celtworld.co.uk May 2011)

Did Jesus Come to Britain? by Glyn S. Lewis
(Clairview Books July 2012)

The Missing Years of Jesus by Dennis Price
(Hay House 2009)

A Complicated Birth by Kyle Roberts (Fortress Press 2017)

Made in the USA
Coppell, TX
03 May 2024